Winner of the Commonwealth Writers Prize for Best First Book in the Caribbean and Canada Region

High praise for *Chorus of Mushrooms:*

"Hiromi Goto expertly layers the experiences of a Japanese immigrant woman, her emotionally estranged daughter and her beloved granddaughter into a complex fabric and compelling story."
Ottawa Citizen

"Such a love for words is evident in *Chorus of Mushrooms,* which contains passages of breathtaking beauty."
The Globe and Mail

"Hiromi Goto, a Japanese-Canadian writer, has written a masterpiece of our times . . . The readability of the text is attributable to the author's craftsmanship, and one feels like reading it over and over again."
The Herald (Harare, Zimbabwe)

"Not only is Goto's language precise and evocative, she has crafted a complex and poetic text that weaves realities and mysteries into a subtle pattern."
Edmonton Journal

NUNATAK FICTION

Nunatak is an Inuktitut word meaning "lonely peak," a rock or mountain rising above ice. During Quaternary glaciation in North America these peaks stood above the ice sheet and so became refuges for plant and animal life. Magnificent nunataks, their bases scoured by glaciers, can be seen along the Highwood Pass in the Alberta Rocky Mountains and on Ellesmere Island.

Nunataks are especially selected works of outstanding fiction by new western writers. The editors of Nunataks for NeWest Press are Aritha van Herk and Rudy Wiebe.

Chorus of Mushrooms

Hiromi Goto

To Holly,

Best wishes on the
path(s) you take.
Kanpai!

NeWest Press
Edmonton

3rd Printing 1997

Canadian Cataloguing in Publication Data

Goto, Hiromi,1966-
Chorus of mushrooms

(Nunatak fiction)
ISBN 0-920897-53-3

I. Title. II. Series.
PS8563.076C5 1994 C813'.54 C94-910167-2
PR9199.3.G67C5 1994

NeWest Press gratefully acknowledges the financial assistance of The Canada Council; The Alberta Foundation for the Arts, a beneficiary of the Lottery Fund of the Government of Alberta; and The NeWest Institute for Western Canadian Studies.

NeWest Press board editor: Rudy Wiebe
Editorial coordinator: Eva Radford
Interior book design: Bob Young/BOOKENDS DESIGNWORKS
Cover artwork: Diane Jensen

This is a book of fiction and all characters are fictional.

Printed and bound in Canada by Best Gagné.

NeWest Publishers Limited
Suite 310, 10359 - 82 Avenue
Edmonton, Alberta T6E 1Z9

For Kiyokawa Naoe. I love you Obāchan.

ACKNOWLEDGEMENTS

In the process of re-telling personal myth, I have taken tremendous liberties with my grandmother's history. This novel is a departure from historical "fact" into the realms of contemporary folk legend. And should (almost) always be considered a work of fiction. Thank you to Kiyokawa Naoe for the stories. Thank you also to Tamotsu Tongu and my family for love and patience.

I wish to acknowledge Kyoko Goto, Yoshiko Gomyo, and Wes Cyr for their part in creating accurate details. I would also like to express my gratitude to Aritha van Herk, Fred Wah, and the strong Calgary writing community for their continued support, and to Mark and Leslie Ellestad for their always encouragement.

Thanks to Multiculturalism and Citizenship Canada and the National Association of Japanese Canadians for funding this project, and additional thanks to the Calgary Japanese Community Association for its support.

The legend is believed, it is remarkable,
and also it is local.

—*Folk Legends of Japan*

1

We lie in bed, listen to the click of blinds, watch a thin thread of dusty cobweb weave back and forth, back and forth, in the waves of air we cannot see. The blankets and sheet are a heap at the foot of the bed, and we are warm only where skin is touching skin. My shoulder, my arm, the swell of my hip. The curve of my thigh. Lean lightly into you. My fingertips are icy, but I am too comfortable to move. To bother getting up and arrange the blankets. I only want to savour the quiet of skin on skin. The murmur of our blood beneath our surface touch. Our breathing unconsciously falls into a pattern, follows the movement of the strand of cobweb that weaves above our heads. You lift your hand to rest its weight, the palm rough, just beneath my breast.

"Will you tell me a story?" you ask. Eyes on the strand of dust.

"Yes."

"Will you tell me a story about your Obāchan?"

"Yes," I close my eyes and breathe deeply. Slowly.

"Will you tell me a true story?" you ask, with unconscious longing.

"A lot of people ask that. Have you ever noticed?" I roll onto my side. Prop my elbow and rest my chin, my cheek, into the curve of my hand. "It's like people want to hear a story, and then, after they're done with it, they can stick the story back to where it came from. You know?"

"Not really," you say, and slide a little lower, so that your head is nestled beneath my chin. Your face in my neck. "But will you still tell me?"

"Sure, but bear with my language, won't you? My Japanese isn't as good as my English, and you might not get everything I say. But that doesn't mean the story's not there to

understand. Wakatte kureru kashira? Can you listen before you hear?"

"Trust me," you say.

I pause. Take a deep breath, then spiral into sound.

"Here's a true story."

Mukāshi, mukāshi, ōmukashi . . .

PART ONE

Naoe

Ahhhhh this unrelenting, dust-driven, crack your fingers dry wind has withered my wits, I'm certain. Endless as thought as breath—ha! Not much breath left in this set of bellows, but this wind. Just blows and blows and blows. Soon be blowing dust over my mummy carcass and beetles won't find the tiniest bit of soft flesh to gnaw on, serves them right. Dust in my joints dry as rust and I creak. Well worn, I am. Well worked. Can't stoop to sweep up the dust swirling in the corners of the rooms. Dust swells and eddies, motes linger to parch my nose, my mouth. Don't bother dusting, I say. It'll come back, surely. Let the piles of dust grow and mound and I'll plant *daikon* and eggplant seeds. Let something grow from this daily curse. But no. Keiko just looks at me from the corners of her eyes. I know. I know. Never mind. No matter. Just let Obāchan sit in her chair in the hall so she can see who comes and goes. My back to the staircase, and I can see who comes through the front door. People have to pass me to get inside this house. Don't try to sneak by, I might stick out my foot. If I look straight ahead I can watch what goes on in half the living room. Turn my head to the right and I see all from the kitchen to the laundry room to the bathroom door. If I tip my head upward, I can see anyone who tries to creak down the stairs. No one moves in this house without meeting my eyes. Hearing my voice. Take no notice, I say. I'll try not to stare. I'll nod and smile. Welcome! Welcome! Into this pit of dust. This bowl of heat. *Ohairi kudasai! Dōzo ohairi kudasai.* Talk loudly and e-n-u-n-c-i-a-t-e. I might be stupid as well as deaf. How can they think a body can live in this country for twenty years and not learn the language? But let them think this. Let them think what they will, for they will. Solly, Obāchan no speeku Eeenglishu. Maybe I'm the fool, but stubborn I am and will remain. Keiko glances at me these days. More often than before with that curl of sour tofu curds lingering in her mouth. I'm not blind. I've heard the talk. "I think we should start looking for a h-o-m-e." As if I can't spell. Eighty-five years old and cast from my home. Ahhh, at least the dust here is familiar. Every grain, every mote as familiar as the smell of my body. No time now to learn new dust in a new home. Let me just sit here. Let me sit here in the hall by the door. There are no windows here to torment me. I can only hear the muffled roar of the wind through the insulated walls and I can drown out the incessant swirl of dust, of chaff, with words. Little songs. And hum.

I mutter and mutter and no one to listen. I speak my words in Japanese and my daughter will not hear them. The words that come from our ears, our mouths, they collide in the space between us.

"Obāchan, please! I wish you would stop that. Is it too much to ask for some peace and quiet? You do this on purpose, don't you? Don't you! I just want some peace. Just stop! Please, just stop."

"Gomennasai. Waruine, Obāchan wa. Solly. Solly."

Ha! Keiko, there is method in my madness. I could stand on my head and quote Shakespeare until I had a nosebleed, but to no avail, no one hears my language. So I sit and say the words and will, until the wind or I shall die. Someone, something must stand against this wind and I will. I am.

I mustn't nod off like that. I must keep this vigil. No, he is still there. Damnit. When did he begin to bother me, this wind? He has always been there, yet I'm certain he did not bother me so much many years ago. When my hair was still dark and long enough to snap smartly like a flag in the wind. And now? Now my hair is short and silver, in tight little curls like a lamb. No wind in here. If I turn my head too quickly, the silver curls tinkle against each other like little bells. Outside, the wind howls and I am silent no longer. Bitter fruit of unripe persimmons. Am I that bitter? No, I am an old woman and I must speak.

Of course there was wind in Japan. I remember so well, the soft spring breeze rustling *midori* green bamboo leaves. *Sara sara sara.* Gentle as wish, as thought and certainly no need to challenge it with my voice. A breath of leaves. My sticky child feet slapping *bata bata* the freshly laid *tatami* sweet as straw. My brother and I drank *miso-shiru* from black lacquer bowls and crunched *daikon* left over from the pickling bins. Still as a pool of water, we were waiting. Waiting for Okāsan to bring our rice and Otōsan to come home. For the cicadas to cry *tsuku tsuku boshi, tsuku tsuku boshi* and the cat to jump up on the verandah. We were waiting as children. Waiting for everything.

Shige and I gathered soft white cloth, string and a

crayon. We pressed cotton stuffing into a ball and twisted the material of the cloth around the ball and tied it so there was a smooth round head and the skirt of the cloth, the body. Just like a little white ghost. We drew in two eyebrows and two eyes, so he would be able to see. Our *teru teru bozu* swung barely, almost motionless, from the rafters outside the house. In the warm wet of summer rain.

Teru teru bozu
Teru bozu,
Ashita tenkini shite okure.

He would charm the rain away and Okāsan would take us to the park. Waiting for tomorrow. The breeze as gentle on my face as my mother's hand. Her fingertips. The green-smelling soil planted with peanuts the day before yesterday and the singe smell of Otōsan's cotton shirts being ironed. We were happy to be waiting then, Shige and I. I could wait motionless for days, sitting on the wooden *engawa*, watching the *koi* make lazy ripples in the pond, the rafters dripping with summer rain. And the rain kept falling into tomorrow.

We had to burn the little white charm. That was the rule. If the *teru teru bozu* couldn't keep the rain away, you burned him.

Pichi pichi, chappu chappu. It hardly ever rains here. Funny how I hated the rain so much when I was a child and now I miss it sorely. A body isn't meant to brittle dry. It's hard to keep the words flowing if you have to lick them, moisten them with your tongue before they can leave your lips. The days stretched long and wet when the rains fell in our childhood waiting. But Okāsan would tell us tales.

Mukāshi, mukāshi, ōmukashi . . .

Okāsan told us tales in our childhood waiting, but the tales she told didn't have the power to save us. Funny how parents tell teaching stories yet they never bother to taste the words they utter. How the words are coated with honey and nectar but the flesh inside is weak and hollow. Let me tell a different story.

Mukāshi, mukāshi, when I was a very young girl, there lived a happy family who was very rich with many storehouses filled to the beams with last season's rice and soft-dried persimmons and the sweetest, smoothest casks of *sake*. There was fresh fish and salted fish and great urns filled with *shōyu* and *miso*. They weren't rich in food only, but had many beautiful things inside the house. There were many rooms and everybody had their own silk-lined quilts to cover them. I never thought of where that silk came from. I knew only that they came from silkworms. And never thought beyond the lovely colours they had been dyed.

I had beautiful dolls to look at and a nurse who held my hand whenever I went outside to play. My brother Shige always followed me, but I didn't mind. He was a quiet boy and he always listened to me. We would dabble our feet in the natural spring right beside the house and suck the water from our toes until the nurse caught us and told our Okāsan. Why, we were rich enough to have a pet when everybody else kept animals for work. We had a dog named Jack, because Otōsan liked Western things. And we were well-respected. People in the village always smiled when they saw us. The villagers smiled with their mouths and I was too young to read what they didn't say in the corners of their eyes. The hollows in their necks. They would bow extra low for our Otōsan, even bow to Shige and me though we were only little children and I felt so important. It was important to me to be important then. I wanted to be like Otōsan.

One day, an extra special day, Otōsan came home early from his office and my, he was so happy! "Okāsan," he said, "please set out my best suit and tie. Shine my shoes as well. The villagers are having a party in my honour." He tried to be calm and serious, but we knew how happy he was. Otōsan didn't have many friends, you see, because he was so rich and had so much land, there weren't many people who were important enough to be his friend. And no one in the village could dress like our Otōsan. He sent for his bank clothes from the capital and he was the only man in our *mura* who wore a bowler hat. Okāsan flushed softly with pleasure to see her husband so happy, and she bustled about to get his clothes ready. I followed Otōsan into his bedroom so I could watch him dress.

"Naoe-chan," my father said to me, "an important man never leaves his home without his *hanko*. You never know when there is a document to sign, a letter to stamp. If someone were to ask you to sign a letter of recommendation and you didn't have your *hanko*, why you would shame the name engraved on it, passed down from fourteen generations." He buttoned his shirt from the bottom, watching his reflection in the full-length mirror that stood in his room.

"Where is my *hanko*, Otōsan?" I asked. "Will your *hanko* passed down for fourteen generations be mine when I grow up?"

"No, silly girl. You will be a lady when you grow up and

you will press the *hanko* of your husband." He smoothed the silk of his tie with graceful fingers.

"Then who will press the *hanko* that carries our family name passed down for fourteen generations?"

"Your brother, Shige, of course."

"But he is much younger than I."

"Yes, but he will be a man some day."

"I'll be a man when I grow up too, Otōsan," I said. "I want to press our family *hanko* and wear a bowler hat."

"I must talk to your Okāsan," he said. "You are much too big to be talking such silly nonsense. Now out! Out! Let Otōsan get ready for his party."

He, dressed in his rich man's suit, his shoes shining with pride, decided to walk to the party so people might see him in his best. We were so proud, Shige and I, that after he left we played going to a party and dressed up in our richest clothes, pouring *sake* into imaginary cups, eating *sashimi* and the tender meat of sweetly stewed eels. Okāsan shooed us to sleep, and we ran *bata bata* on the *tatami*, to dream of *hankos* and bowler hats.

Easy for a child to believe in the powers of her parents. When there is food and song and happy myths told long into the night. When you sleep beneath blankets made of silk. I could only trust what I had known in the house of my father. I could not know that we were privileged. That people hated us for our wealth and power. I could not know that loss and pain were as easy as one *hanko* pressed in red ink. One stamp on a legal document.

"Shhhh, *shizukani.* Naoe-chan. Pack your cotton kimonos. No, leave the silks, they are too fine. Quickly, now. Quickly!" Okāsan so strange and it's not even morning, the sun isn't up and grey and cold. Her eyes so strange and glittering. "Okāsan, what—" She slapped me. For the first and only time in my life she slapped me. "Pack your clothes. Be silent." I didn't cry, just packed the clothes my mother had heaped on my *futon* and stood where she told me to. "We must leave," she said. And the words were like stone.

One *hanko*. The family seal. Kiyokawa. The simple characters of our family name engraved in ivory and passed down for fourteen generations, our home, our mountain, the land, one stamp. Kiyokawa. Pure river. Ha. Even the purest river can be polluted, and it will be. It was. The villagers plied our Otōsan with sweet words and sweeter *sake*. They lulled him with compliments and begged him to sing and to share with them his wisdom. They tricked him into signing documents he was too drunk to see. I am not bitter. The home, our mountain, the land, all Otōsan's by right of a seal. The pain and the hardship of the villagers who only rented the land they had worked for fourteen generations but never owned for their labours. I am not bitter for losing something that was unevenly divided. The things I missed, the things gone forever, were the sweet smile on my Okāsan's face, the silly stories Otōsan made for me.

"Otōsan, where does the breeze come from?"

"The breeze comes from the sky. He gets so tired of being blue, he sighs in discontent."

"Otōsan, where does the wind come from?"

"The wind comes from the clouds. They are making silly faces and trying to blow each other away."

"Otōsan, where do the storms come from?"

"They come from the demons. There are not enough bean cakes to go around, so they are having a farting contest to see who is to win them!" Otōsan pronounced with a serious face and I was serious in my belief. Okāsan was sewing a *yukata,* but she dropped the films of summer-thin cotton to laugh and laugh, her hand politely covering her mouth. And baby Shige laughed with her, even though he was too young to know why.

One *hanko*. Pressed in red ink. Dulled with rice wine. One *hanko*, and everything gone.

Who has left that screen door unlatched? The wind is shouting against the door frame, hurling insults at this house, my home. Slap, bang. Slap, bang. *Tomare*! A cup in my hand. It has always been there, smashes against the door. Shatter. Keiko. My words are only noises in this place I call a home.

"I thought that you didn't learn how to speak Japanese until after you grew up," you say, tapping your finger on your lips.

"That's right," I answer. Pull the string for the blinds and crank open the window. The room is stuffy with our sleep breathing and the tang of love and sweat.

"Then how do you know what your Obāchan said? I thought you couldn't speak with her when you were growing up in Nanton. Or did I get it wrong?" You watch me dig through the laundry hamper for some not-so-dirty clothing. I turn a pair of panties inside out and slip on a pair of your jeans. Roll up the cuffs.

"No, that's right," tug a white T-shirt with no logo over my head.

"Then how can you be telling a true story if you never knew what your grandmother said?" you ask. You are still in bed, the blanket around your belly. I sit down on the edge of the bed to smooth doubt from your mouth. Lean in, and dip my tongue between your lips.

"I'm making up the truth as I go along."

Naoe

Keiko is dusting. Scattering dust so it settles everywhere else, polishing doorknobs, scraping the frame above the door. What for? No need, I say. There is nothing as silly as dusting when you live in a desert. But she ignores me. Keiko. My daughter who has forsaken identity. Forsaken! So biblical, but it suits her, my little convert. Converted from rice and *daikon* to weiners and beans. Endless evenings of tedious roast chicken and honey smoked ham and overdone rump roast. My daughter, you were raised on fish cakes and pickled plums. This Western food has changed you and you've grown more opaque even as your heart has brittled. Sliver-edged and thin as paper. I love you still. You are my daughter, after all, and this you cannot change. For all that you call me Obāchan and treat me as a child. I am not your grandmother. I am your mother.

"Obāchan, please! I want to clean this hall. Can you just go upstairs so I can clean up this hall?" Keiko rolls her eyes backward so she is staring up inside her ketchup brain.

"Nanio yutteru ka wakarimasen. Nihongo de hanashite kudasai," I say and she grinds her teeth and refuses to understand the Japanese she spoke twenty years ago. Child after my own heart, I suppose. We are locked together perfectly, each pushing against the other and nothing moves. Stubborn we are and will remain, no doubt. She yanks the vacuum cleaner out of the closet and swirls the dust even more, trying to suck up everything in her path, cramming the head between the legs of my chair, running over my feet until I move them out of her way. I could laugh, I suppose, if I weren't so stubborn. There is little hope left

for you and me, Keiko. We choose our words and speak them with little time for thought. I know. I know.

"You're an old fool," Keiko whispers, and clatters the vacuum cleaner after her stiff spine. I nod and smile. *Onnajida yo*, Keiko, *onnaji.* We are the same.

Ahh, easy to lose track of days, of years, when a chair becomes an extension of your body. I wasn't born in this chair, and I won't die in it, that's certain, but I have room enough to think here, and almost nothing can sneak past my eyes. I may be old, but I'm not blind. This chair can serve me still and I needn't move at all. My words will rattle around me. I speak my words, speak my words, and I say them all out loud. I yell and sing and mutter and weep from my seat of power.

The wind is not as strong today, so I needn't shout. Only mutter. If there is nothing to obstruct the wind, would I still hear it? I wonder. I have a piece of dried salted squid in my pocket and I tear a bit off. I must chew and chew. Like beef jerky, but much tougher. I chew and the juices begin to fill my mouth. It gives me energy, this squid, the more I chew, the tastier it gets.

"Where did that come from?" Keiko so mad. Always a peak to her obstinate upper lip. I nod and smile.

"Keiko mo dōzo itadaite kudasai," I offer and raise some shrivelled squid legs to her pointing finger. Her lips turn white and she slams the kitchen door behind her. There is enough slamming of doors with this constant wind. It is Shige and his wife who send me the packages, of course. Poor, yes, but kind and they send me a package now and then. I may be an old fool, but stupid? Surely not. I have my own box at the post office, but you don't know, Keiko. I

pay for it with the coins I collect from the couch cracks after dark.

Naoe Kiyokawa
Box 2909
Nanton, AB
TOL 1RO CANADA

This pit of dust. This bowl of heat. Salted squid. They send me salted squid. Not always, because it is so expensive, and *osenbei.* Crisp rice crackers dipped in soya sauce, I crunch them in bed at four in the morning. It's Muriel who sneaks the packages up to my room when everyone is asleep. My granddaughter, your daughter, Keiko. You taught her no words so she cannot speak, but she calls me Obāchan and smiles. She brings the packages and we crumble the *osenbei* together in my narrow bed. Muriel does not suit her, Keiko. I call her Murasaki. Purple. She cannot understand the words I speak, but she can read the lines on my brow, the creases beside my mouth. I could speak the other to her, but my lips refuse and my tongue swells in revolt. I want so much for someone to hear, yet it must be in my words. So stubborn, so clenched I spite my face. Damn you wind. Howl! Howl!

Murasaki places her head in my bony lap and I begin to speak my words.

Mukāshi, mukāshi, ōmukashi . . .

• • •

A girl opened a door, balancing a paper brown parcel on one arm. An old woman sat in bed. A huge pillow propped her up, but her head hung low on her hollow chest, wheezed heavily with the breath of age. The young girl set the box on the floor beside the bed and reached down, touched her grandmother's cheek with two fingers. The old woman nodded. Slowly opened her eyes. She smiled, stroked her granddaughter's hand, gestured toward the box and said, *Akete chyōdai.* The girl knelt on the dust-creased floor and quietly picked at the tape on the package.

Outside, the wind screeched and the seams in the walls funnelled the dust into growing wedges. The girl slid her thumbnail along the crease of the masking tape. Sound of tearing. The old woman watched, her eyes traceless of the sleep she had woken from. The young girl flipped the heavy cardboard lid back on itself, all four sides, and reached into the box. Plastic crinkles, crackers dipped in soya sauce, lightly fried, crackle crunch between teeth, and flat leather sea squid, tentacles twisted and wrinkle-dried so tough to chew until the ball, the socket of the jaw aches but the juices linger salt and sea. Tiny crocks of pickled plums, the brine so strong the mouth drenched with a passing thought and look! a bottle wrapped in plastic and paper and plastic and paper and black character on the label. The grandmother smacked her lips, *Sake!* and the girl looked up, saw the old woman's eager mouth, and smiled because she could taste how sweet the *sake* was from her grandmother's face.

• • •

Murasaki

I could still taste the *sake* lingering in my mouth. Licked my lips again, to trace the last drops. Obāchan smacked her lips. Mom always ragged on her to cut it out, how rude she sounded, but it's really appropriate to smack lips. It's like a symbolic gesture of respect to what you've consumed—how truly wonderful it is to swill the *sake* in your mouth, rolling it on your tongue, letting it drip drop by drop into your eager throat. Smack, smack. Ahhh. That was good.

Smack, smack! (Obāchan)
Smack, smack! (Me)
Smack! Smack! (Obāchan)
Smack! Smack! (Me)

"Obāchan, cut that out! We're trying to sleep in here!" Mom yelled from her room. Dad groaned, only waking up because Mom was yelling across his face. Obāchan and I looked at each other and started cackling. She pulled the blankets over our heads and we snorted into her crumbly sheets until we ran out of air.

"Obāchan, we've got to stop eating those rice crackers in your bed."

"*Sonna koto kamau ka? Koyatte Murasaki to isshoni iru koto ga ureshii no yo.*"

"Obāchan, why do you call me Murasaki?"

"*Anta ga jibun de imi o sagashite chyodai.*" She smiled, reached for the *sake* bottle and tilted her head back to catch the last drops on her tongue. Soaked it up. I snagged a piece of squid from the box and popped it into my mouth. There're two ways of eating squid. To chew and chew and chomp and chew and wring out the juices from the leather flesh, or to hold the squid in your cheek and let it soak up the saliva slowly until it swells and softens. Obāchan always chewed like mad, words falling out with each snap of her jaw. I held my words inside my mouth until they swelled and softened.

We ate, we drank, in Obāchan's bed of feasts. Now I was tired and all roasty toasty, covered in sheets of cracker. I snuggled my head in Obāchan's bony lap and closed my eyes to listen. I couldn't understand the words she spoke, but this is what I heard.

Mukāshi, mukāshi, ōmukashi . . .

Listen, Murasaki, listen. Do you wonder why the wind howls like a stricken woman? Do you wonder why the rain sometimes tastes like blood. *Che!* The Greeks. Forget the Greeks! And don't quote Bible verses to me, child. There were stories long before Eve tasted fruit fit for women. Yes, stories in each blade of grass, flesh of worm, drop of dung. They linger and grow and only women to reap them. Let the stories suckle your breast, they'll ease the ache within you. Don't come to me for answers, child, these are only words. Nothing an old woman has to say carries much weight in this dust dry wind. Words will flake and wither. Yet I speak still, the words, they will spew even if I clench my teeth, meld my lips in revolt. But these stories are not for you I speak them, but for whoever I will. I am. Come, sweep the crumbs from my bed and lie down beside me. There, that's nice. Much warmer with two and the words will keep us company. If someone should knock on the door, we'll welcome them into this bed of tales.

Of course, there was a time when I was grim and

silent. It's only when you are truly beaten there is nothing to say but breath.

When the wind wails like a woman and rain tastes of blood, it is time to remove your skin and fall naked from your body. This wind. So little rain when the wind is static dry. When I stoop and shuffle with the scritch of slippers, the electricity builds in my wire body, my hair floats, a white aura, and I'm afraid to touch. If I went outside, lightning would collect about my head, thunderclouds about my feet. But I've never left this dusty house, it hasn't been the time.

(Murasaki: How long have we been in bed, Obāchan?

Naoe: I don't know.

Murasaki: How long will we stay in bed, Obāchan?

Naoe: Child, I don't know.)

You wonder who sends me these packages, don't you. These "mystery packages" you call them. You cannot read the characters, only trace the lines with your finger. Childhood sweetheart, you read. Aging lover. No, a woman whose life you saved when she flung herself off the platform and you grabbed the back of her coat and the train roared by, inches from her face. No, child, no. These packages, these gifts are sent to me from your great uncle, my brother, and his wife, Fumiko. Yes, there was a time when I was a child and had a baby brother. Now he is as withered as I am worn and his wife, Fumiko, no longer plants *daikon* and eggplant seeds in the garden. They pluck cobwebs with their fingers and weave the thread into tiny tapestries, light as breath, as thought. They tell each other tales, when they gather threads together. Bent of spine, silver hair yellowed by motes of dust, they stir like quiet mummies in the corners of the rooms. So lucky for them, they are two. One can begin forming the words, the other listening, and if the one who speaks should tire, the other is there to finish. They tell each other legends, myths. They re-create together.

Mukāshi, mukāshi, ōmukashi, arutokoroni, ojiisanto obāsanga imashita. Kono ojiisanto obāsanwa taiso binbodattasona—
(Naoe: Do you hear what I say or only what you want?)

Mukāshi, mukāshi, chisana murani, ijiwaruna bōzu ga imashita—
(Naoe: Will you listen with an open ear and close your eyes to thought?)

Mukāshi, watashiwa—
(Naoe: What are you waiting for?)

I can't. I can't. Ican't. Ican't.ican't.ican'tican'tican't

I stop.

I turned my head slowly in Obāchan's lap, the fabric scratch and stiff. Inhaled dust and poetry. She stroked my forehead with her palm and her words, they flowed fluid. I snuggled close, curled my legs and stopped pretending to understand. Only listened. And listened. Then my mouth opened of its own accord and words fell from my tongue like treasure. I couldn't stop. Didn't try to stop. They swirled, swelled, and eddied. The words swept outside to be tugged and tossed by the prairie-shaping wind. Like a chain of seeds they lifted, then scattered. Obāchan and I, our voices lingered, reverberated off hollow walls and stretched across the land with streamers of silken thread.

Naoe

Words, words, words, WORDS. Ahh, words grow heavier every day, upon my bony back. My body folds over itself under the weight. My back groaning, *akiramete*. Give up. You crush your crinkled spine with the stones you drop from your mouth, hurl from your gut. I sew my lips together with a curved needle, but the words seep from my nostrils, my ears, even leak from my paper dry eyes.

"You sit there and mutter and taunt me in Japanese just for spite," Keiko hisses from the crack between the kitchen door and frame, one eye stabbing me through the tiny space. It is not so, Keiko, but the door has already clicked shut before I can explain. Why. Even I don't know, sometimes. The words of an old woman can change little in this world and nothing of the past so why this torrent of words, this tumble of sounds such roaring, sweeping, chanting, sighing. Hummmm. I only know I must.

Gawa gawa gawa gawa
Oto tatete
Are are mori no mukō kara,
Soro soro detekuru hikōsen.
Marukute annani hosonagaku

Banana no yō ni fukuranda
Fukuro no naka ni wa nani ga aru.

We learned it in kindergarten. Yes, we had kindergarten, eighty years ago, in Japan, where I saw my first blimp. A zeppelin. Something huge and floating. A song to commemorate a blimp. We, filled with wonder at something so huge, so solid, floating above our heads with the roar of heated air. We clapped our hands and ran squealing after the silly brown balloon, our teacher chasing us. I asked her about the words in the song.

"*Sensei*, the blimp is not yellow," I said.

"No," agreed my teacher, "it is very brown."

"But why, in the song, does it say the blimp is filled up like a banana? The blimp is brown and it isn't even shaped like a banana."

"It is only a song, Naoe-chan, and the words aren't that important. We are happy to see the blimp and we sing a merry song," she smiled.

"But it's not true. We are singing a song, but the words are not true."

"If you leave a banana out in the sun for a long time, it turns brown, you know, Naoe-chan."

Gawa gawa gawa gawa . . .

There was not enough money for me to stay in school. Such a pity, the teachers said, you're such a clever girl. Never mind, you'll do all right, you're such a clever girl. But there was not enough money for books.

I went to work at a silk farm. They looked at my hands, my back, the size of my legs and sent me to the growing barns. There, the silk worms hatched from pin-prick eggs. We were their nurses. Fed them, changed their sheets of mulberry leaves, fed them, sorted them, fed them. When they were tiny, tinier than eyelash or breath, we had to mince the mulberry leaves with great knives. The leaves stained our hands green sweet. No one talked, this nursery of extravagance. Each woman, each girl keeping the unwritten silence, and the only sound thousands upon thousands upon thousands of miniscule jaws munching in ferocious appetite. Each night I dreamt my body was covered with squirming, munching, defecating worms, wriggling into my nose, my ears my eyesmymouth. Screamed. Until Okāsan came and touched my face with her cool hands. The dreams did not last. My body tuned to the rhythm of the worms, their weekly sleep, two days, then shedding skin and growing growing. I even grew to like them, hairless, cream white and soft as the skin on a baby's neck. Sometimes, I cupped grown worms, thick as my finger, in my hand and lifted them to my cheek. Skin the scent of mulberry leaves. Thoughts of infant pigs and green rabbits. Our job was finished when they wrapped themselves up with their precious thread. We piled them on trays like so many quilted eggs and they were taken away. Our work was done.

One cocoon in my pocket.

I save winter moths from Keiko's vacuum cleaner. I tuck them into the folds of my clothes, and when everyone is asleep I mix sugar with water and feed them from the cup of my palm.

There are ages of silence and ages of roaring. When I was young and beautiful, my lips were an ornament upon my face. Now my face is crumpled with care and seams adorn my cheeks. My mouth bursts wide and the words rush out, a torrent of noise and scatters. An old woman on a wooden chair might not be much to look at, but step inside her circle of sound and fall into a tornado.

I was married, once, to a man, then we divorced. Most unheard of, fifty years ago, in Japan. And Makoto was the one to cry when the final papers were signed. When it was he who sought the comfort of a priest's daughter, so young and tender, she didn't see the weakness around his mouth, his eyes, until it was too late. For her. He was not all to blame, of course. I can sit here now in this bowl of heat and touch the memories with cool fingers. I can see the attraction of a young girl's love. A young girl's adoration. Limbs so slim and breasts so young they would melt on your tongue. A girl too young in experience to know the weakness some men carry. I did not envy her youth or her beauty. I did her a wrong, because she gave me the reason to leave a marriage I never chose to enter. And she to enter the space Keiko and I left behind us.

"Naoe," he whispered, "come to me." I left the comfort of my *futon* and crawled beneath his blankets, face rigid and spine stiff. He was not unkind. His hands were warm and gentle. Perhaps if he had placed his lips upon mine, covered my mouth with his and breathed some blood back into the roots, but it was not the fashion to kiss and I was not willing to part my lips. He parted my *nemaki* with careful hands and touched my breasts, my thighs. It was not unpleasurable, this touching, and I was always ready when his body covered mine, but I never moved to touch him and I never said the words. Just the beat of blood in my temples chanting, "I did not choose to marry. I did not choose to marry."

Choices made remain unchanged and useless to wish it otherwise. Choose now! I shout, Choose now! The wind howls, forces dust through seams in the walls, and swirls a dry web around me. Choose! I scream and dust turns to mud in the pit of my throat. But that cannot stop me. I ball the mud with the back of my tongue and spew it out with the force of my words.

"Hssssst. Naoe. Not married yet? My, oh my. Old Miss, Naoe. You're nothing but an Old Miss. Juices all dried up and nothing fresh left. You're leftovers. The shop's closed and nothing left except shrivelled plums and dried out apples. Better hurry, Naoe. Better hurry, or your Otōsan will have another thing to cry about. You poor thing. It's almost too late."

I didn't care. I really didn't.

Old fool. Of course I cared, or I didn't not care enough. I did get married after all. Could have refused, could have stayed home, could have swung from the rafters by a long silk cloth. Could have—I thought about all of these things and more, but there they remained. As thoughts. I acted on nothing and my lips only opened to scream when Keiko was wrenched from my body with great gleaming hooks.

"Otōsan, where does pain come from?"

Keiko and I, our differences remain. But there are times when one can touch the other without language to disrupt us. Daughter from my body, but not from my mouth. The words we speak leave small bruises on the skin, but what she utters from her face doesn't always come from her heart. Sometimes, we are able to touch the other with gentle thoughts and gentler hands. We still have our hair days, and she still asks me to clean her ears. Such a fragile trusting thing, to have one's ears cleaned by someone. It's not something you can ask of everyone. It is more a woman contact, something that boys grow out of. But old women will turn to their daughters to have their hair looked after. Grown women will still turn to their aged mothers and ask to have their ears cleaned. As long Keiko asks me to, I know she trusts me.

I am an old woman, and I am also stubborn, but that doesn't mean I'm stupid and bitter. It's only that I spent so much time saying nothing in my youth, I have to make up for things unsaid in this house of dust and moth.

There are so many moths this year, it's all the rain we had this spring, some say. I wait for them, each night, to flutter from the wrinkles in my clothes. People are so silly about moths. Keiko bats her hands around her head, crushes them with wadded Kleenex, or sucks them up with the vacuum cleaner. "Dirty, filthy insects," she says. Murasaki plops empty cups over them and slides a piece of paper underneath so she doesn't have to bear their frenzy of wings against her skin. She tosses the moths outside and they flutter back toward the light. I cup them in my palms and stare. They are as furry as mice given dusty wings. I would like to stroke the fur on their bodies, but my trembling hands are clumsy. So I only hold and look. Whisper. They stay and listen for a while and flutter away with the whir of beating wings.

You carry the groceries in from the garage, the bite of minus thirty-seven degrees Celsius cutting through the warmth of the kitchen faster than you can close the door. I set the last pot on the draining board and dry my hands.

"Did you shut the garage door?" I ask, and you shake your head. I stick my feet into your large snow boots and plod awkwardly outside. It is so cold that the automatic garage door is incapable of being an automatic anything. I have to press the button, then reach up to grab the rim of the door to drag it shut. Only I am stupid. So stupid. I didn't bother to put any gloves on and the pads of my fingers are still damp from washing dishes. I am stuck to the garage door with my hands above my head and the wind is tearing like knives into my back.

"Help!" I yell, stuck between crying with cold and pain and laughing at my own stupidity. "H-h-h-help!" I laugh/cry and you stick your head around the corner.

"What's wrong?"

"I'm stuck to the garage door, my fingers, they froze on the door," I gulp, warm tears rolling down my icy face, laughter bursting from my lips like gasps. You are amazed, never having seen a human actually freeze and stick to something. You rush to my side, breathless with concern. And I watch, mute with horror and fascination, as you open your mouth, extend your tongue, to lick my fingers free. Steam rises moist from the warmth of your mouth, but the warmth is nothing compared to the icy strength of an Alberta winter day. Your tongue freezes to the garage, just above my fingers.

We are so pathetic I am laughing and laughing until I can't stop. You start laughing too, but it rips at your tongue making your eyes water. Hot salty tears drip down your face, land on your tongue, my fingers. You laugh only to cause yourself pain. So that it makes you cry long enough to melt the ice that holds us.

You soothe a balm on my fingertips and there is nothing to be done for your tongue except to stroke it with some of the sticky flesh of the aloe vera plant.

"It's a bit bitter," you muddle, around the pain and stickiness in your mouth.

"Do you want me to kiss and make it better?" I ask.

"No! Thank you. Just go on with your story so I don't have to think about how much my tongue really hurts."

I blow on my fingers and settle my head in the warm cup of your thighs.

Murasaki

Obāchan's bed of tales was a good place to dream in. Her words sometimes notes of music instead of symbols to decipher. Lay my head in her bony lap and swallow sound. There are worse places to be when you are thirteen. Of course there were times when my Mom and I had conversations. But the things we spoke of never lingered in my heart or deep inside my head. She couldn't offer me words I craved, and I didn't know how to ask.

It's easy to travel distances if you fly on a bed of stories. My Mom didn't tell tales at all. And the only make-believe she knew was thinking that she was as white as her neighbour. I wanted to hear bedtime stories, hear lies and truth dissembled. I wanted to fill the hollow with sound and pain. Roar like the prairie wind. Roar, like Obāchan.

(Naoe: Child, here is a story for you. Somewhere to begin.)

Mukāshi, mukāshi, ōmukashi . . .

When there was nothing but the primeval waters, Izanami and Izanagi left their celestial home, crossing a bridge of many colours.

"Where are we going?" Izanagi called to his sister, who strode ahead of him.

"We are going down," Izanami answered. The bottom of her robe staining blue and green and violet from the seeping bridge.

"But there is nothing down there except oily water,"

Izanagi cried, lagging further behind.

"Hurry! Or the bridge will fade out from under your feet."

Izanagi looked back, and sure enough, the bridge was slowly fading, its colours evaporating like mist.

"How will we go home?" the boy panted, running a little to catch up with his sister. He caught her hand and held tightly, looking back once more, to the growing pace that separated them from the glowing lights of their heaven.

"It's time to make a new home," a smile began to form on Izanami's lips.

"How can you make a new home? There's nothing down here except black water," Izanagi argued, twisting his fingers inside Izanami's cool grasp. He was angry with his sister who had taken him from his comfortable home. He had been eating gingko nuts, and now he was sorry he had not brought any with him, for there would be nothing to eat in this oily water except a few unsightly jellyfish, most unpalatable unless dipped in hot pepper and sesame seed oil.

"We are gods," Izanami said, dropping her brother's hand. "We can create."

"Oh," Izanagi was a little taken aback. "What are the rules?"

"There are no rules," Izanami chanted, and saying it aloud made it so.

They reached the foot of the bridge where the colours seeped into the black water, little rings spreading blue, green and violet.

"This water is displeasing. I wish the water to reflect the color of the sky." At her words, the water rippled and spread away from where she stood, a growing circle swelling outward until all the water hummed a singing blue.

"That's nice," Izanagi sighed.

"Now it's your turn," his sister said.

"Let there be light!"

"No! No!" Izanami shouted. "That's not the way to do it. Take it back!"

"You said there were no rules!" her brother complained in his normal voice.

"I said there were no **rules**, but there is such a thing as good taste and understated beauty. Make this *mittomonai* light go away," Izanami said. "Besides, the sky and water aren't blue anymore. You made them turn into a sickly olive colour with that awful light."

"Okay, I take it back," Izanagi muttered. The sky and water turned blue again and the sickly bright light disappeared.

"Now it's my turn," Izanami said.

"No fair! You cancelled my light so I should get another turn."

"No, if you botch your turn, you've used it up. Besides, we have to hurry. The bridge is almost faded and we still don't have anything to stand on." Izanami stood, tapping her foot on the last wisps of rainbow beneath their feet.

"All right," Izanagi muttered. "But hurry up. I'm getting hungry."

Izanami dipped her fingers in the cool blue water and flung the droplets back into the water. "I wish for green islands, like jewels, to rise from the sea," she chanted.

"Don't forget the gingko trees," Izanagi said, poking his sister in the ribs with his forefinger.

"And gingko trees like giants to reach and embrace the sky."

The droplets of water congealed, swelled, growing green and healthy. Bursting with mountains and valleys and the rush of waterfalls, the squeak of gingko bark growing. Izanami and Izanagi stepped off the almost faded bridge onto the firm, green-smelling soil of the new island.

"Nice," Izanagi sighed.

Beneath the arms of a great gingko tree, they collected the fallen fruit. Izanami and Izanagi told each other tales as they peeled the outer smelly flesh and roasted the inner nuts in the embers of a fire. They pushed the nuts out of the low blue and orange flames with a stick. Picked them up, still too hot to handle, burning their fingertips and tongues in their eagerness to eat them.

(Murasaki: Obāchan, this story. Is this a story you heard when you were little?

Naoe: Child, this is not the story I learned, but it's the story I tell. It is the nature of words to change with the telling. They are changing in your mind even as I speak.)

Mom never told me of her childhood stories. There is a hollow in my hearing I must fill on my own. Not like Obāchan, who breathed words in and out all day. Mom's voice only rattled like a tiny mushroom in an otherwise empty bucket. Her stories must be ugly things filled with bitterness and pain. The pain of never having told. And Dad, the man who unlearns with the ease of breath. His is a physical response, like a knee-knock-swing or sneezing after looking at the sun. He is as blameless as a chameleon changing colour. Yeah, sure. Obāchan, yet. Obāchan, still.

You hover about my ears my eyes, you touch the things I care to dwell in.

Yet.

Mom and Dad made me work at the mushroom farm. An odious job, literally, when you are a child. They wanted me to learn about responsibility and patience and forbearance and how money must be earned and not taken for granted and other basically fundamental Baptist attitudes. I hated it. The sour stink of compost and the armpit smell of mushroom soil. No kids but me, and they made me do jobs that were most boring and most meaningless.

"Girl," Joe said, "go make boxes."

I hated him. Calling me girl and making me make boxes. Hated the way cardboard scraped against cardboard in that raspy squeak and the hair on my arms stood up and prickled up my neck and not in a pee-your-pants-feel-good-way either.

"Girl," he said, "go do blocks."

I hated him. Calling me girl and making me set blocks between every post of every bed of mushrooms. Doing the dumbest job on what everyone called the Green Machine. A huge assembly line that took a stack of beds on one end then jerked them down the line, one by one, for either spawning or loading or casing. Why it was called casing I'll never know. All we did was cover the spawned shit with peat moss. Where did the cases come in? And me with the dumb job of blocking every post with a four by four cube of wood so that the spaces between the beds would be bigger. Wider. Running around the bed to get the four corners, then punching the button so that the bed was crammed upward piling them on top of each other sometimes six high when the forklift was too slow in coming back and it all teetering and the fear of it toppling and crushing me stupid and no way a hard hat would save me even if I was wearing one. Calling me girl.

"Girl," he said, "break."

"Muriel, some Boat People are coming to work on the farm," Mom said.

"What do you mean, Boat People?" I asked.

"They are people who left Vietnam because it's a difficult place to live because Communists have taken it over and the standard of living's been so reduced that they just can't bear to stay. Or for some people, it's too dangerous to stay. And they had to sneak away on boats, because it is against the law to leave. Be very nice to these people, Muriel. They've suffered so much."

"Oh," I said, not thinking beyond the words I heard. No, I was doing something. Doing this thing of adventures at sea like the *Medusa* and wondering about the gory details of people drowning and what happened when there was nothing left to eat. I wasn't immune.

"Help me think up of some nicknames for these people," Mom said, "their real names are too hard to pronounce and no one will be able to remember them."

"Okay," I was eager, the thought of thinking up new names for grown-ups gave me a thrill of pleasure. I ran my finger down the row of names, rolling foreign words on my tongue. Changing them. "How about Jim?" I asked. "How about Joe?"

"Joe," Mom mouthed. "Yes, that's nice and simple. Joe it is."

"Girl," Joe said, "phone."

"Girl," Joe said, "pick room twelve."

"Isn't that being steamed?" I asked.

"Steaming it tomorrow," Joe said.

"I don't think I should have to pick it. It's not worth the effort. All I'll get is a couple of crates of diseased number twos. Only worth a buck a pound. It's not worth it," I stood my ground. For my picking rights.

"Ohhhh?" Joe said, in his annoying way. "You the boss now, girl?"

Grabbed buckets off the shelf, cling clang rattle and muttering muttering beneath my breath. "I'll *girl* you, you asshole. Make me pick in the fuckin' junk room all by myself. Fuckin' stinks in here. Ah, god! There's nothing in here but stinkin' number twos and green mold! Why do *I* have to bother with pickin' them for fuck's sake. They should just steam this sorry mess and be done with it. But, no. Make the boss's daughter pick the stinkin' room by herself." So busy filling my ears with bitter, I didn't hear what Can was saying. He might have been saying something else, but all I ever heard was Joe calling me girl.

I didn't enjoy working at the mushroom farm. I simply didn't enjoy working. All the pickers talking Vietnamese and laughing, I was sure, at my slow picking. Everyone'd be done three of their rows and I would still be on my first. Whoever finished their own rows would have to loop back and pick toward me, so I wouldn't be left behind when everyone went to the next room. Sometimes, if the next room had to be picked before the gills opened and turned them into number twos, I'd be left on my own. No sound except the plipping of water into puddles on the floor, then the sudden intermittent explosion of the furnace starting up, so loud in the mushroom hush of darkness, I'd squeak out loud for fear. I would push the mushrooms down, through the soil, and cover them with peat moss so they were completely buried. Buried hundreds and thousands of mushrooms so that I could leave my silent tomb. If there were simply too many to bury, I would go and sit in the outhouse for hours on end, watching spiders drug flies and then suck out their innards.

It was difficult growing up in Nanton, daughter of a father who grew mushrooms, daughter of a mother who became an other, granddaughter of a grandmother who never shut up until she left the house forever. It's difficult growing up, moving closer then farther away from people who tell you they love you. I'm not bitter. I'm just saying, it's difficult growing up. People say this and that.

"You're lucky to be a kid growing up in a time like this. When I was younger, only very rich people could eat bananas."

Sure there are plenty of bananas to be had now, but I don't even like them. And when you start thinking about who picks them and who pockets the money, you're lucky if a lump will even get past your lips. You have your basic Yankee Doodle Tom Sawyer role model, but let's face it: most childhoods begin and end in Cinderella's ash heap. People say, "Oh, I would just love to be a child again." But I would never go back to that fairy tale.

Home life is something you have to cart around with you forever. No Freudian shit for me, but the home life stuff gets tattooed on to you something awful. Or something good. Just depends. Hysteria or history can become one and the same. Passed on from daughter to daughter to daughter to daughter to. . . . The list is endless and the tattoo spreads.

You're born and things stick to you. Some fall off, but most you carry around for the rest of your life. Let me be old and foolish when I grow up.

Naoe

The wind blows from the west, the west, the west, again. Shrieking from the throats, the very teeth of the monstrosities they call mountains. From the bowels of the sea, the moisture sucked onto the jagged peaks, only dust left to blow across this prairie bowl. But sometimes, the wind swirls from the south and takes an easterly curve. I can smell the compost, then, from the compost barn. If they are turning the compost over, the smell is ammonia acrid. I have never been there, to the compost barn. I have never seen the mushrooms growing. I have never left this chair.

Keiko used to come back from the barns smelling like soil and moist. Like birth. I used to press her clothes to my face and breathe deeply, smell-taste her day. Warm semen smell of the first crop of mushrooms, wet wet peat moss, the tepid coffee she drank at 10:00, the stink of formaldehyde she used to sterilize her buckets. I can see these things with a scent in my nostrils, a passing taste on my tongue.

Easy for an old woman to sit in a chair and talk and talk. Easier, still not to say anything at all. I could nod and smile and watch "Sesame Street" so I can learn French as well as the English people don't think I already know. *Bonjour!* I'll say and everyone will be amazed. *Je m'appelle Naoe Kiyokawa.* Ha! If an old woman sits in a chair and never gets out and talks and talks and talks, don't ignore her. She might be saying something that will change the colour of your eyes.

Dai Makoto. His name was Makoto Dai. Is, I suppose, he's still alive, so I hear. I had to put Kiyokawa aside, the name to flow through my brother's blood, to the child they never conceived. Dai Naoe. The words written on the marriage document made it so. Lucky for me I changed my name before I came to English. The spelling different, but the weight of the word in sound would have been burden enough to plague me. Naoe die.

An easy thing to change a name. All it takes is ink and a piece of paper. A whole dimension on a family tree erased when one name is dropped and another assumed. All those mothers and daughters and mothers and daughters swallowed into the names of men. It would make us tear our hair, beat our breast, if we thought about it long enough. Enough of this tree nonsense! *Mattaku!* Leave it already, I say. Who cares what your father's father did and who was given what honour. Honour dies with the person who earned it. Don't leave me a bowl of rice in a golden shrine, don't waste oranges on my memory. Bone crumbles. Flesh melts. If a few words I uttered were to echo in someone's mind, then that is enough.

Makoto was not a bad man, and I did not despise him, but he was weak and foolish. He was not completely to blame, of course. I was proud, proud as only a daughter of a once rich man could be. And he was an easy one to torment.

"Naoe," he called. "*Sake.*"

I heated the *sake* until it boiled over and the alcohol evaporated. Until it turned as sour as vinegar.

"Naoe, this *sake* is overheated. Be careful next time."

Next time I barely heated it at all, as tepid as cooling urine.

"Naoe, it's too cool this time. You must have more care."

I overboiled it again. Bottle after bottle, I never said a word, served vinegar and urine until he lay on the *tatami* seeping *sake* tears, begging me to get it right, while Keiko watched with round black eyes.

"Okāsan, why is Otōsan crying?"

Nothing. I said nothing. Piled small bowls, dishes, *tokkuri, ochoko,* ivory *ohashi,* cluttered to the kitchen. Too tired, too angry to heat water to wash them, only left to harden in the tub, scurry of cockroach, one cockroach seen meant ten unseen, Keiko tugging my sleeve, my *obi,* Makoto crying so weak like Otōsan, Keiko tugging, and me saying nothing nothing NOTHING. I threw the *futon* down from the cupboards and made up our blankets. Keiko lay between us. Her Otōsan weeping and I, I was a silent *katamari* of hate.

Such a great anger I had. I hated for so many years. Am I angry still, I wonder and stretch my hand to feel.

It's sadly unfortunate that I was too angry to enjoy sex when I had it. Too bitter, too proud to fall into my flesh. Long after the divorce, I still wouldn't let anyone touch the surface of my skin. Not even Keiko. Now I pay, I suppose. Eighty-five years old and horny as a musk-drenched cat. The only human contact I have now is when Keiko washes my hair. When Murasaki sometimes hugs me. I love them and their touch makes my old heart almost pain with emotion, but there is nothing for this dull beating ache I find between my thighs. Most unseemly, to be this age and horny, but it is funny after all. This muttering, old, lamb-haired Obāchan wearing elastic-waisted polyester pants, brown collarless shirt with pink flowers, grey cardigan and heel imprinted slippers. Just pulling out the waistband with one quavering hand and the other just about to slip into cotton briefs, toying with the idea of—

"Obāchan! What are you doing?!"

I release the elastic and it snaps back to my wrinkled stomach with a flat smack and Keiko standing in the doorway with her mouth open. I start to mutter an excuse, but Keiko's expression, my elastic pants, my horniness, my age, I start laughing and laughing until the old muscles in my stomach start to ache. Ahhh Keiko, it is funny after all.

"Sam, I think Obāchan's finally gone senile," Keiko hisses. Funny how the dark can carry sound so lightly. Even above the whistling creak of the seams in this house. Squeak of bedsprings. Shinji's faced the wall.

"You've been saying that for the last ten years," he mutters. He's tired after loading compost all day. The smell was especially acrid this afternoon.

"She was doing something strange today," Keiko whispers. She's lying flat on her back, staring up at the ceiling. "So what?" Shinji hisses. "Kay, I'm tired. I don't want to hear about your mother tonight, all right? Just let me get some sleep."

"She started to stick her hands inside her pants, but I caught her in the act and she stopped and started laughing," Keiko continues, ignoring him.

"Really?" says Shinji, rustling blankets and the creak of bedsprings. Now he's facing Keiko, suddenly interested and not at all disgusted. "I wonder why?"

"I told you! She's going senile. I read somewhere that when some people go senile they start soiling their pants like babies and smearing their feces all over themselves, or even eating it!" Keiko, all horrified and disgusted. "I think I'll call Silver Springs Lodge and ask about the waiting list. I just can't deal with feces."

"Maybe her crotch is itchy," Shinji suggests.

There is a gurgle in my chest, up my throat, and at the back of my mouth. I bite my blankets to muffle the sound but snort through my nose instead.

"Sam! Obāchan's choking!" Flung blankets, *bata bata* of bare feet on hardwood floors, sudden white light, and squeeze my eyes shut, still snorting through my nose. Shinji pounds my bony back and Keiko is trying to pry my eyes open with her fingers, why on earth for? And I unclench my teeth and the blankets fall out and I laugh and laugh and laugh.

I am tired, some days more than others, and today I am tired weary. Not even enough energy to mutter, the words seep out like breath. Bury me not, on this blown prairie.

It is hair day.

Keiko is moving one of the kitchen chairs into the laundry room. It is the most *atatakai* room in the house because of the heat from the dryer turning, the sun through the window. If it is not summer, parched and gasping, it is an endless winter of tiny ice crystals crinkling through the seams in the walls. Gets into my knees, my toes and slows the blood. But it is *atatakai* in the laundry room and my blood does not freeze clumpy inside my wrinkled veins. I'm not so proud that I can't enjoy the pleasure of someone's fingers in my hair. I'm not so stubborn now that I can't fall into my flesh. The wind will howl, but a body needs to look after her hair sometimes. Keiko doesn't say anything at all, and I only have to hum, watching her bustle from my chair in the hall. I can see all the way down through the kitchen into the laundry room. I can even see the washroom door. She says nothing out loud, but she moves the shampoo and conditioner to the large sink and the soft-nubbed brush. I put my two hands on the seat of my chair, beside my bony thighs, to push up my hollow buttocks. Whooosh, I breathe, and lean forward in a stoop. My back is bent and my belly is pressed up against my spine. Eyes spin, then settle. My slippered feet are stiff with cold from being still for hours. Or decades.

I wander from my chair, from my hall, with the scritch sluff of dust between my slippers and the hardwood floor. Down the hall, into the kitchen where I can smell stewing pork and boiled potatoes. I say nothing to Keiko, only hum softly between my lips. *Gawa gawa gawa*.... Through the kitchen and finally into the laundry room. Ahhh, she's not forgotten the yellow stool for my legs. It's most unbearable for a body's legs to swing above the floor, all the weight hanging from the knee, blood pooling in the feet like stones. I creak back, into an unfamiliar chair, warm hum of the dryer turning, soothing. The *atatakai* sun on my face. My feet on the stool. I close my eyes, the pleasure of touch magnified when I feel without my eyes.

Keiko's soft, middle-aged belly leans into my shoulder. Warm and soft, like *manto,* I feel my stringy muscles loosen their hold on my bones. Her belly absorbs my pain. She softly rubs my brow with her palm and runs her fingers back into my scalp. Keiko's fingers in my hair, through my hair, on the tired skin of my head. Ahhhhhhhh. She rubs small powerful circles with her fingers and thumbs, the tension rising up, off my head, floating upward like angels to heaven. Fingers strong and firm, pressing thumb in that spot where my neck and head meet. The press, ease, press, ease, of fingers of thumbs through my hair, on scalp, on aching scalp, slow rotation. My temples, slowly, her fingertips are strong, her touch so soft, down, across aching eyes, softpress my eyelids, down nose, around cheekbones, and finally, easing, easing my overtaxed mouth. She rubs and rubs my overworked jawbones, so tough, so stubborn, they could knock down whole cities if someone were strong enough to wield them. Keiko has finished massaging and she wipes my face with a hot towel, so that when the heat evaporates, it takes with it any remaining aches.

I lean my head back, into the sink. Rest my head on the towel Keiko has placed on the rim. Hmmmmmmmm-mmmm. The steady rush of water, Keiko checking the temperature on her wrist, warm water streaming, not a drop on my face or ears. Just warm water, moisture filling the tiny laundry room and the scent of Keiko's clothes through my closed eyes. Snap of shampoo cap. Green smell of apples. She warmed the shampoo so it is not sudden and cold on my scalp, and lather begins to fill her hands, her fingers easing the itches from my skin, my pores. Keiko cups one palm beneath the back curve of my head, holds the weight in her hand. With her right hand, she rubs vigorously, with the pads of her fingers and a hint of fingernails. Not scoring the skin like an amateur, but a vigorous, generous scrubbing. From my hairline to the base of my neck, she scrubs side to side and backwards at the same time, her soft belly, a pillow for my shoulder. She doesn't miss a single itch and she finds for me and washes away itches I don't know I have. Warm water streaming away the soapy suds, not a drop on my face or ears. My eyes still closed. Squeak of clean hair. Conditioner, like warmed heavy cream in my silver curls. Keiko works it in with her fingers first, slowly and carefully, then the soft-nubbed brush. Soften skin. My body limp and moisture filling my skin, I don't know if I can ever open my eyes again. Keiko rinses again, water hotter now warming my head, my face, my neck, the heat and moisture embracing my body, my pleasure, the *atatakai* sun.

My hair glows. Filaments from a silk worm.

The winter is hard on my winter moths. The sugar water, the canned peaches, not enough. Each night a few more die, a few more fall from the folds in my clothes. The brown patterns on their wings fades and the fur falls from their shrunken bodies. "Thank you, Naoe, for the peaches. Thank you for the sugar water," they whisper. I smile. This dying is a natural thing. And their eggs are somewhere, hidden like treasure.

My sleep is a place uncluttered of dreams. Who was that silly Chinese philosopher? The one who fell asleep gazing at a butterfly and dreamt that he was a butterfly dreaming that he was a philosopher. And when he woke up, he didn't know if he was a philosopher or a butterfly. What nonsense. This need to differentiate. Why, he was both, of course. Thoughts impress on soft skin and a taste can linger for days. Words tumble from my mouth and change shape and size. They grow arms and legs and crawl about in the dust by my feet, pick up dried moths with curious fingers and scrabble at my pant legs. I feed them with stories and they munch and munch. They grow bigger and stronger and walk out the door to wander over this earth.

The slow heaving shudders of this planet we call *chikyū.* This spinning mote, again, circling the sun, always circles spinning ever. The pattern has been set long before the sister and brother, Izanami and Izanagi, left their celestial home to create the world. Japan. Yes, Japan was the world, a long time ago when people called what they could see with their eyes, the mountains, the trees, lakes, and stones. The very soil beneath their feet. That was where their world began and where their world ended. Japan. Island to itself and don't leave your home. Easy to be convinced of your strength if there is nothing to compare it to. So much pride on such a little island, nowhere to go except to blow outward. No room for change except through death. And death. The cycle repeats itself. I sit here now, so far away and look back with eyes that see. At least now I see with some distance so my eyes have room to focus. Certainly, I read the newspaper, heard talk on the radio. *Ara-raaaa.* I said. *Ara-maaaa.* There will be war. Not knowing what it meant.

We lived in Manshū and Shina for ten years, Makoto and I, and Keiko too when she was born. Never returning to Japan in all that time, only once, for Keiko's birth then back again, finally when war broke out. Ten years and I never learned to speak Mandarin or Cantonese or any other dialect. I stayed behind the walls they built around the cities, the towns, to protect the people who lived there from the people who lived without. Makoto building bridges across rivers and chasms. He even convinced himself that he was working for the betterment of the Chinese people. To aid in their development. Stupid fool. The bridges were for Japanese soldiers to march across to kill their inland cousins. And I was the stupidest fool of all. I never questioned why the schools were made separate, why Chinese and Japanese were not taught together. Why Chinese children had to learn Japanese, but Japanese children were not taught the words of the land they lived in. Why there were servants in our modest homes while there were people starving outside the walls of the city. The words of one woman would not have turned the marching boots of men, but the pain of not having spoken, of not bothering to ask questions, still aches inside me now. When I became the wife of Makoto Dai. Bitterness turned inward and I didn't care for the things around me. Not even Keiko.

Winter in Manshū, and the wind. Snow like salt and the sting of cold chapping red hands and feet. Breath shattering, trying to light the stove, to cook rice, urine retreating far up the bladder, too cold to come out. We were more privileged than most of the Chinese people. Our home was modest, but we could still afford house help. We had a boy who lived with us. Fetched winter-wrinkled *daikon*, limp *hakusai* and eggs from the market. Made soup. He woke up early and knocked the rim of ice from the top of the water tank and washed our sheets, our underclothes in water still slushy thick with ice. Ironed our clothes and folded blankets and all this while Keiko was strapped to his back with strips of cloth. I huddled beside the tiny stove and mended clothes until my fingers split with dry and cold. When Makoto was away, building his bridges, the boy sat at the table with me to eat. He told me stories and I could almost understand.

"It is the responsibility of the men in developed countries to aid their underdeveloped brothers," Makoto stated, filled with sour *sake* and self deceit. The boy poured the soup carefully.

"My work here is done. We're moving farther south in the spring to build bridges across the whole country! The bridges will be a symbol of good will between our people and the Chinese." Makoto, so proud and foolish. More fool me, for not uttering words of doubt. For not asking for another truth. His bridges echoed with the marching steps of thousands upon thousands of Japanese soldiers. They crossed his bridges of goodwill to slaughter their inland cousins.

We left the boy and his soup and his stories in the almost spring, and travelled by train to Shina. His name. Did I ever know his name? Did he ever tell me or did I never learn it? Filthy black soot seeping into pores and dust speckling against the door. Black soot and dust. Dust and dust and wind and dust! Will this wind never cease? Will this dust ever settle? Keiko wedges Kleenex into the cracks beneath the door, but the wind whispers in somehow. Cold eddies around my ankles. It makes a body wonder how dust can fly even in the middle of winter. Air so dry the lining of my nostrils split and crack. Bleed. My lips, two scars upon my face. Still, the words, they come.

"Obāchan, would you clean my ears?"

I just hum and rise from my chair, shuffle to the living room to sit on one end of the couch. The sunny side. Keiko's face relaxes, the tight muscles beside her mouth lose their ache and her lips look soft and full. She lies on her side and rests her head on my bony lap. She hands me the *mimikaki* and I peer into her ear.

"Ara — ippai aru janai no. Yoku kikoeta ne."

"I know," Keiko says, her voice husky, "do it softly."

When the wind swirls from the south, takes an easterly curve, it brings with it a scent of rich moistness. The dust does not fly where the mushrooms are growing. The air hangs heavy with wetness. Shinji comes home with mushrooms seeping from the pores in his clothes. The scent, so *fushigi*, so mysterious.

"Hi, Grandma. How was your day?" he says in English. Every day.

"Māmā no toko da ne."

"Glad to hear it," he says, no matter what I say. Once, I said I spent the day masturbating with my toes. Another time I said Keiko scrubbed the walls with shit and wiped the floor with piss. But all he says is, "Glad to hear it." I suppose if a body can learn a new language in twenty years, you could unlearn one as well. No, Shinji has truly forgotten the language he left behind. I can accept this, but Keiko is another matter. A child from my heart, a child from my body, but not from my mouth. The language she forms on her tongue is there for the wrong reasons. You cannot move to a foreign land and call that place home because you parrot the words around you. Find your home inside yourself first, I say. Let your home words grow out from the inside, not the outside in. *Che!* But I shouldn't point my finger. Shouldn't behave like I've never let anybody down. Especially Keiko. Another stupid circle and no end in sight, I suppose. I'll never forgive Keiko in words and she will never utter to me the words I wish to hear. We love each other in noisy silence.

Shinji is not a man like my father or my husband. Keiko certainly didn't err in her choice of a partner. Shinji is a simple man, so hard to be simple in this cluttered world filled with dust and howling. To choose a simple life over an easily cluttered one, something pure must remain. One cocoon wrapped in silk. A pocket of eggs. Soup.

A different soup in Shina, and a new boy. What was his name, how could I forget his name? I slept with a pistol beside my pillow, for people hungrier than I were on the other side of the wall. Keiko always with the boy, always clinging to the hem of his shirt or a sleeve or pocket and he didn't scold her. Keiko never coming to me because I did not answer. My thoughts sour as dust. Makoto away, making his paper bridges, "For my inland cousins," he said. I did not go to the market. I did not tend the garden. I did not change my *kimono.* I did not wash my hair. I wandered around the house with a brush in one hand and a pot of black *sumi* in the other. Went from paper screen to papered walls to skin-thin windows and wrote my name in tiny characters.

清川　直恵　　　清川　直恵　　　清川　直恵　. . .

The boy. . . his name is Sui Mintan! Yes. Yes. The name begins the story.

Keiko is at Lucky Dollar. Buying pork chops and steaks and macaroni and cheese. What I wouldn't do for a nice *chawanmushi!* Steaming delicate egg custard, but without the sugar. More like a delicate egg souffle. Steamed egg in a cup, if you will. A tender-firm shrimp on top and all sorts of surprises inside. Why, you can find *shiitake,* or scallops or *takenoko* or spinach. Anything at all, or all at once. But it's the gingko nut I crave. Always one, in the bottom of my bowl, Okāsan never forgot. The squeak of the plump nut between my back teeth and the mealy green taste. Okāsan used to fry them in salt and oil, with the nuts still unshelled. And Shige and I peeled them when they were still too hot, cracking the thin shell between our teeth and burning our tongues and fingertips. Grains of salt in the creases of our lips. We drank water until our bellies were as tight as drums and then lay on the sweet *tatami.* Rolling a little from side to side, to hear the water slosh.

During war, there are no thoughts forever. Three things only: Is there water? Is there food? Who is still alive?

Gisei...and Sui Mintan says leave, you must leave and I know that that is what he says, the words, the sounds that spill from his mouth say leave because there is danger for you and Keiko, and Makoto conscripted, walking over the very bridges he designed, that he built for his inland cousins, only now he has a gun in his hands and a belt filled with bullets and Keiko and I we leave, we leave and join Shige and Fumiko and Otōsan in Pekin and Otōsan too weak to travel, too ill to travel from Pekin to Kinken to Manshū to Chosen to Hong Kong to Japan, so very very far away, and Otōsan says you must leave while there is time, no need to wait for the old to die when there is time for the young to live, take Keiko home, home to Japan and Shige and Fumi can watch over me and you and Keiko will be fine and remember and grow, and we leave again, again, always leaving and the train and the dust and the wind howling with war and the gas masks we clutch in our hands, the ship, the life jackets, the nauseous fear of mines unseen beneath the choppy waves or submarines or bombs falling from the sky and thinking of Otōsan and Shige and Fumiko still in Pekin, *kinchyono katamari, daijobukana, demo shinuka ikirukato harao kimete yatto Nihonni tsuite, Nobeokani kaette Makoto no Otōsanga mukaeni kitekurete,* よう無事で帰ってこれたねぇ。 みんなで心配しちょったよ。 And he hugs us, hugs us close and my bitter dry eyes grow wet. We send a telegram to Pekin, to Otōsan, we are fine and back home, in Japan, we are fine and Otōsan reads the message, his hand shaking, smiles, and closes his eyes for the last time.

But we are not fine. There are rumours that Americans will soon invade Japan by boat, and the people, the villagers, the old people, the children, the wives, we chop bamboo from the groves and slice them at an angle, sharp as bayonets, to spear the enemy when they land, only they come, they come, not from the sea, but thunder in the sky above us, B-29s, huge, swollen with their cargo, in deadly formation, dropping destruction. Fire bombs, pitching sheets of incredible heat, melting everything, even metal, even stone. The fire roaring and swelling, cresting like a tidal wave to engulf us all and I run, I run, I run with Keiko clutched under one arm and a thin blanket to cover our heads, to the bomb shelter, the shelter, I run, the heat crackling the air around us snapping whipping the roar, the roaring winds of fire.

And when the fire dies

We creep from the shelter

We stand in the embers of our homes and only ask,

"Is there water? Is there food?" and "Who is still alive?"

Gisei. That is what we called Hiroshima and Nagasaki. Those people. The children, the infants, the elderly, the women.

Sacrifice.

Murasaki

The daughter of a daughter of a daughter of a daughter of a daughter of a daughter of a daughter of ... the list is endless.

But I am here.

I turned my head slowly in Obāchan's lap, the fabric scratch and stiff. Inhaled dust and poetry. She stroked my forehead with her palm, and her words, they flowed fluid. I snuggled close and curled my legs and stopped pretending to understand. Only listened. And listened. And then my mouth opened on its own accord and words fell from my tongue like treasure. I couldn't stop, didn't try to stop, they swirled, swelled, and eddied. The words swept outside to be tugged, tossed by the prairie-shaping wind. Like a chain of seeds they lifted. Scattered. Obāchan and I, our voices lingered, reverberated off hollow walls and stretched across the land with streamers of silken thread.

I stand in the wind. I face the wind. It blows my hair. I like it. I am six.

I can talk. I can talk anything I want. Try and stop me.

"Me Chinese, me play joke, me go pee pee in your Coke! Hahahaha!"

"But I'm not Chinese," I protested.

"Yes you are! You are! You are! You're a slanty-eye Chinaman. Hweee chong chop ching Ahhh so! There, what did I say just now. Tell me what I said in Chinaman."

I was confused.

"What are you, stupid or something?"

"No, *you're* stupid!" I yelled.

"Am not!"

"Are so!"

"Am not!"

"Are so!"

"Am not!"

"Are so!"

"Fuck off Chink. Who needs you?"

"BUT I'M NOT CHINESE!"

These are hysterical stories.

God! Did I just make that up or is it true? I don't even know anymore. Saying it out loud can make it so. I never kept a diary. I'll make it up now and put in the dates later. I'll write with my left hand and call myself Hank.

Look, here's another airport story.

I met this guy at the airport in the departures area. Where are you going, he said. Japan, I said. Back to the 'ole homeland, huh, he said. I just shrugged and smiled a bit. You know, he said, you're pretty cute for a Nip. He said. Most Nips are pretty damn ugly. All that inbreeding. Even now. He said. Well, have a good one. He said. And boarded his plane. And I felt really funny inside, him saying Nip and everything. Because he was one too.

Obāchan, what? You are ninety-one years old? One hundred and five? If anyone could live that long and still wander over this earth it would be only you. Old woman of moth and dust. Is it ever too late to learn? Obāchan, I learned to speak Japanese after you left. Because I wanted to. It's a good reason. And you know what I learned, Obāchan? I learned that there's no way to say I love you in Japanese except to a spouse or lover. Not to your sister or brother or daughter or son or aunt or uncle or cousin or mother or father. Or grandmother. All you can say is *Daisuki yo.* A tepid, I like you very much. But I'm glad I learned Japanese because now I can juggle two languages and when there isn't one word in English, it will be there in Japanese and if there's something lacking in your tongue, I'll reach for it in English. So I say to you in English. I love you, Obāchan.

Love is a strange thing. Stranger the older I grow. When I was an adolescent, I could never picture myself getting married to a gorgeous blond man and living with him forever and ever amen. So what happened? I fell for a fresh-off-the-boat; actually, he flew in on a Boeing 747, a Japanese man fifteen years older than me. He liked to arrange flowers. This is not a stereotype. And he did it amazingly well. Snip, snip. Snip. The lower leaves of a peony stem. The flowers were still tight and beads of nectar pearled on the buds. Ants were everywhere. Not that they particularly bothered me.

"Hey!" you interrupt, "are you talking about me?"

We are driving southbound on Highway 2, driving from Calgary to Nanton to visit with my Mom and Dad. My Mom loves you so much, she would eat you up if she could.

"This is a story. One of many." I look both ways down the railway tracks that cut across the road without even slowing down. Whip past High River in the wake of a semitrailer.

"I know," you say, "but you said they were true stories."

"Listen, they're true if you believe them."

"Is that logical?" you ask, reaching for a cassette tape of Japanese enka music.

"I don't know. In fact, I don't really care if it is or not. Does it bother you that you're in the story?" I glance over to you, eyes leaving the highway. I know every curve, every dip, every speed trap on this eighty-five kilometre stretch.

"No," you pop out Talking Heads to put in Misora Hibari. "Well, I don't mind as long as you don't make me look stupid."

"I'll make you look great," I promise. "Anyway, it can't really be you once I make it a story. It becomes someone else, you know?"

"Not really," you say, "but keep on going."

"Are you sure they'll blossom?" I asked, my bare feet on the chair beside me.

"Yes, they'll blossom. And smell very sweet."

"I'm not convinced," I said, watching him. Snip, snip. Snip.

"Wait. They will flower in a few days."

"Where'd you learn to arrange flowers?"

"A Buddhist monk taught me."

"No shit?"

"No, no shit. He lived in an old temple and the wood is always damp and mildewed. Very dark too, inside, and thick with mold and incense. He lived by himself, it was a small country temple, and slept on the *tatami* with only a thin *futon* to lie on. One night, after he had chanted all his *okyō*, he lay sleeping in the damp. In the dark. Just when he was almost falling into sleep, he felt this tickling tickling crawling up his leg. He almost twitched but suddenly awake and thought, 'Centipede!' Ha! Don't laugh. You only have tiny infant centipedes in Canada. Especially Alberta. Too cold. But centipedes can grow huge in Japan and a big one's bite can kill even a baby!"

"No shit?!" I was getting excited. Not sexually, but by the story.

"No, no shit. So my *sensei* lay very very still and he felt sweat trickling from his shiny bald head and his testes shrivelled up with fear because this centipede is crawling crawling up his body. But he is a very strong man so he doesn't move, doesn't move and up and up over his belly and chest and a c r o o o o s s s s his neck and slowly slowly crawled off his body, one leg at a time. It took a very long time." He picked up the last peony stem. "And when the last leg stepped off his neck, my *sensei* leapt to his feet, very quick he is for his age, sixty-eight, and turned on the lamp and saw! A centipede one metre long! Hurtling across the *tatami!*"

"Oooooh, god! No way!"

"Yes way! He looked for something to catch it with, but the floor was bare and when he looked up, the centipede was gone." He was finished. The tight buds of the peonies looking hopeful, a cluster, a triad, a sweeping stem nodding. A balance that almost collapses. It was beautiful.

"Do you want to fuck?" I asked.

He just took my hand.

The ants go marching one by one. . . .

We stayed in bed for a fortnight. I've no idea how many days that is, but that's how long we stayed. We ordered pizza and Chinese food and threw a rope out the bedroom window so we wouldn't have to get out of bed. We tossed crumpled fifty dollar bills and yelled, "Keep the change!" Everyone called back, "Enjoy! Enjoy!" And we did.

The sweet scent of peony blossoms. He was stroking infinity on my nipples when I heard a thud.

"What's that?"

"What's what?" he asked, infinity turning to stars.

"That," I said. Thud. *Para para para.* Thud. *Para para para.* I looked over his shoulder to the flower arrangement on the teak display table. The heavy blossoms were falling off the stems and the breeze from the open window was scattering the petals.

"Your flowers are toast," I said.

"That's all right," he said. "If I'd wanted to keep them forever, I would have drawn them."

"What? You draw too?"

"I also paint," showing me. And again.

We could have met anywhere. We could have met, say, in an airport.

"Are you a tourist?" he asked.

"Why?" asking back, "why do you ask me?" I looked down on myself, my sneakers, my jeans, my Mickey Mouse T-shirt. The cigarette I had tucked above my ear fell to the floor and I picked it up and brushed the filter off with my knuckles. I slipped it between my lips and patted my back pocket for the lighter. He produced his without fuss or flourish and lit my cigarette.

"Am I dressed like one or what?"

"No," he answered, "it's not the clothes you're wearing. It's the way you smell."

"Jesus!" I raised my right elbow ear level and sniffed my pit suspiciously. Nothing too bad. I'd smelled plenty worse. "Jesus," I repeated, "you some kind of weirdo or what?"

"You smell different," he continued, "I can't tell whether or not you've just arrived or if you're about to leave."

"Jesus!" I repeated. "What country am I in anyway?"

(Murasaki: Obāchan, are you listening?

Naoe: Yes, child, always.)

When I was little, so very little, my Mom made me go to Sunday school where I learned

Red and Yellow, Black and White
They are precious in His sight
Jesus loves the little children of the world!

There were pictures drawn on the song boards too. Indians with feathers and black boys with curly hair wearing only shorts and yellow people with skinny eyes. And a blonde girl with long eyelashes with a normal dress on.

"Everybody is the same," the teacher said, "Jesus doesn't see any difference at all. He loves you all the same."

I thought that Jesus must be pretty blind if he thought everybody was the same. Because they weren't. They weren't at all. Sometimes, there would be a Guess Speaker, a missionary from deepest darkest Africa or from a head-shrinker tribe in the Amazon. There would be a slide show of before and after natives and a display table of primitive tools and graven images. Everyone would get to touch these things as a reminder that godless places still exist.

At Christmas time, there was always a brown paper bag for each child. Mostly peanuts very cheap, but a scattering of coloured mints. And a Jap orange.

"We thank you Lord, for this wonderful Jap orange. A marvel of agricultural technology. Aren't the people truly clever."

When I was little.

What is there to say about a voiceless man? All that is unsaid. My father's space inside my thoughts is dim and unformed. He could coax mushrooms to grow in the dust-strewn prairie and convince badgers to eat from his hands, but he never sat beside me to fill my ears with nonsense. He lived on his skin surface and I can't even remember what he smelled like.

Dad was a living mystery, one I couldn't decipher. How could he employ over twenty people and hardly say a word? He spent so much time in his office, I was convinced he was completely lazy or working magic spells. How else could a man who barely spoke convince moist mushrooms to grow in a desert? He left almost everything up to Joe and signed cheques once a month after Mom had done the bookkeeping. Sure, he wandered around the damp hallways, whistling a melody of something I couldn't recognize. Looked into a few growing rooms and turned up a thermostat or two. Sure, he delivered the odd truckload of mushrooms to Calgary. Sure, he came into the coffee room at ten in the morning and three in the afternoon and sometimes at six for a bought-for-take-out supper from Ginger Jim's when the picking would continue on past ten at night. It wasn't like he sat around at home all day watching soaps. But he spent a lot of time in his office and I never asked to go inside.

(Murasaki: Obāchan, are you safe, are you well? Not sleeping on pebbles or eating nettles or sucking on snow for moisture. Where are you now, tonight?

Naoe: Child, I linger here.)

"What's that funny smell?" Patricia asked.

"What smell?" I asked. "Can I have half of your Wagon Wheel?"

She broke the Wagon Wheel, the marshmallow stretching a bit when she pulled the halves apart. She gave me the bigger half and nibbled on the biscuit, licking the chocolate away.

"That smell. Your house smell."

"What house smell?" I said anxiously. We didn't eat foreign food at all. Only meat and carrots and potatoes like everyone else. And Obāchan hadn't sneaked any squid for months.

"It smells like warm toes or something."

"Is it gross?" I asked. Clean warm toes or dirty ones?

"No, not gross," she thought, picking at the marshmallow with her pinkie. "Just funny."

"I can't smell it," I nervously glanced around my house with new eyes. Strange to me for the first time.

"Don't worry, you smell something all the time and it's like not smelling anything at all. I don't know what my house smells like," she smiled reassuringly.

"Potato steam."

"Is it gross?" she asked. Curious.

"No, it's just potato steam."

"Do you want to play outside?" she licked chocolate smears from her fingertips.

"Sure."

I wandered in my house after that, my nose a finger pointing. And really smelled for the first time. I didn't want to believe that our house had a smell. And Mom was so clean all the time. From cranny to closet I scurried about, hands on my knees and all hunched over. Obāchan said,

"Kore, Murasaki-chan. Nani o shiteru no ka na?" as I scuttled to and fro, from kitchen to hallway to living room closet.

"Not now, Obāchan, I'm looking for something." I crept back and forth, then crawled to my grandmother. Sniffed cautiously around her ankles.

"Ara ma ha! ha! ha! ha!" she laughed. *"Mattaku inu to*

sokkuri! Nani o isshōkenmei sagashiteru no?"

No, it wasn't her. Obāchan only whiffed slightly of dust and the sweet smell of chinook. Warm toes, warm toes, nose and nose and nose warm toes. Some lingering odour from the laundry room. I poked in the laundry hamper, filled with Dad's work clothes. And the waft that rose around me. The clamour of mushrooms growing.

I was horrified. Something so insidious tattooed into the walls of our home, the upholstery in our car, the very pores in our skin. We had been contaminated without ever knowing. For all that Mom had done to cover up our Oriental tracks, she'd overlooked the one thing that people always unconsciously register in any encounter. We had been betrayed by what we smelled like. We had been betrayed by what we grew.

You know what I hated most? Valentine's Day. Those press-out Valentine card booklets that everyone bought, including me, and I knew what I would always get. At least five of them. Every year. I hated it. The press-out Oriental-type girl in some sort of pseudo kimono with wooden sandals on backwards and her with her hair cut straight across in bangs and a bun and chopsticks in her hair, her eyes all slanty slits. I knew there was something wrong about me getting these cards. What the picture was saying. But the words weren't there to speak out loud yet and all I could do was feel this twisty thing inside me. I only smiled and said, "Thank you," like my mother had taught me. And burned them when I got home.

"Happy Valentine's Day," Dad said, and gave me a heart-shaped candy that would crumble in my mouth tang-sour that said, YOU'RE MY SWEETHEART. Mom gave me two dollars and Obāchan winked.

(Murasaki: Obāchan, are you cold?

Naoe: No, I'm full up with ginger and hot sake!

Murasaki: Wait a minute, Obāchan. Just stay a while.

Naoe: Something you want to talk about, Murasaki?

Murasaki: Obāchan, everyone wants to hear stories. And I can't finish them. They scatter like sheep. Like dust.

Naoe: No need to tie them up. There is always room for beginnings.

Murasaki: And I've been doing this thing where I bite the inside of my mouth accidently and it swells up so that it's even easier to bite and it swells even more and it never has a chance to heal and I bite again and again. Obāchan?

Naoe: Yes?

Murasaki: Will you tell me a story?

Naoe: I thought you were tired of tales.

Murasaki: Never of hearing them.

Naoe: I'll tell you a tale of "*Uba-Sute Yama*"

Murasaki: Is this a real story?

Naoe: As real as these words here and now.)

Mukāshi, mukāshi, ōmukashi . . .

When it was so very difficult to find food in plenty, there lived a poor, poor family in a poor, poor village on a poor, poor mountainside. The village was so very poor that there was a law decreed that upon reaching your sixtieth birthday, you must be abandoned in the mountains by your family. Well, there was outrage and anger and plenty of tears, but the younger people were secretly pleased because parents who were sixty years old were too old to watch over five children and cook dinner and weed the garden and haul water, but young enough to eat two bowls of barley gruel every day. So there began a practice of carrying one's parent on the back to the ritual place of abandonment.

Now there was one grandmother who was fast approaching her sixtieth birthday, and every day, she counted on her fingers, counting down the days. "Well," she thought, "well, I might as well do a nice home perm before I go."

(Murasaki: Obāchan, did they have home perms so very long ago?

Naoe: Well, they do, indeed, in this tale I tell you now.

Murasaki: I like that. I like that notion.)

So the not so very old but fast approaching sixty-year-old grandmother walked, *sa! sa! sa!* up mountain down mountain across a creek with her bare feet to her sister's house for a home perm. *Sa! sa! sa!* She walked walked walked. "Where are you going?" people called, raising their heads, backs still hunched over in the endless cool mud ache of replanting rice. "Where are you going, Obāchan, in such a hurry?" The grandmother only pulled her lips inside her mouth and grinned quite grossly, mimicking toothlessness, and waved with a flap flap of wrist, not pausing for a bit of gossip or a sip of cold boiled water.

"Ara-raaa. Yappari," the people muttered into tender blades of rice, "It's her turn now and she's so frightened that she has no words to talk."

At last the grandmother reached the house where her sister lived. Her younger sister was cleaning the mud from her straw sandals, sluicing her icy calves with water from a bucket.

"Older sister! Why it's such a long walk to *wasa wasa* come and see me. Please sit down. In the sun where it's warm and I'll go and put on some hot water for us."

"No fuss. Don't fuss." She squatted on her haunches by the doorway and, "Whooosh," sighed. Rocked a little on her heels and seeped forward back toward her toes. Her younger sister hung her wet scratchy sandals from a peg in the wall and stumped barefoot into the house. There was a clatter clang of lid on kettle and the hiss of cold water poured into an already hot *nabe.* The grandmother could hear her sister raise this lid that, rustling clatter of boxes, jars, and empty containers. Heard her sigh. She came out holding a well-chipped and slightly heat-warped wooden tray with two cups of hot water. And nothing else.

"I'm sorry, *Onē-san,* this is all I can serve you."

"No fuss, don't fuss. Ahhh, this hot water is fine! I was

thirsty after my climb. No, no, I came to see you and ask a favour."

Her sister knelt on the ground beside her, bowed low until her straggle hair was streaked with dust. The grandmother stroked her sister's knobby back and waited. Her sister looked up with tears in her eyes.

"Ara-raaa. Now why are you crying? I've come to have some fun!"

"Fun?" asked her younger sister. The word strange on her tongue.

"Yes, fun. Now up! Up! We have to get ready," the grandmother said, her eyes merry as minnows. "I want you to give me a nice home perm."

"I'm so sorry. We had to trade my home perm set. I don't have it any more," her sister said, miserably.

"No matter! No matter! I'll think of something, that's certain. Let's go!"

"Oh no, I couldn't!" said her younger sister. "I still have to stoke the fire and the twins will wake soon and my son and his sons and my daughter-in-law will come home in half an hour waiting to be fed and the bath to fill and heat and I haven't even—"

"When was the last time you had fun?" the grandmother asked.

"Oh, well, I guess, it's been a long time."

"How long?"

"Over fifty years."

"Then it's time to have fun again," her *onē-san* said, and held out a work-scrabbled hand. So they left the twins, the empty bath and climbed up into the mountain. They walked some time, just holding hands, the trees as warm as stones.

"Why, I haven't done a nice home perm since I don't know when! But what will we use for curlers?"

The grandmother stopped, winked and reached down to the cushy forest floor and held up a pine cone.

"Pittari!" her sister laughed and clapped her hands. They chattered and collected pine cones together. When they had enough, they found a tiny glade of bamboo where the sun trickled. Sat close like they did when they still lived in their mother's house.

"I have a surprise for you," the grandmother said, smiling. Smiled again.

"Oh, what?" Her younger sister cried, clapping her hands like when she was a child. "What, oh what is it?"

The grandmother reached into her sleeve and pulled out half a package of Mild Sevens, a lighter, and a Meiji chocolate bar.

"Oh, *Onē-san,"* her sister sighed, eyes all dreamy. The grandmother tucked a cigarette between her sister's lips and lit. Lit her own and broke the chocolate bar in half. They flopped backwards on the springy moss, and drew deeply on their cigarettes. Nibbled on chocolate between puffs of heady smoke. Looking skyward at the flickering blue between bamboo sheaves.

"Are you having fun?"

"Yes."

They lay silently. Only the sigh of smoke trickling into lungs. The smack smack of tongue and lip on pieces of sweet chocolate.

"Are you scared *Onē-san?"*

"Of what?"

"Of *Uba-Sute Yama?"* the younger sister said, with a small shudder.

"Not at all," the grandmother said, smacking her chocolate.

"Why not?"

"Because what we call something governs the scope and breadth of what it'll be." The grandmother sat up and clasped her arms around her knees.

"What do you mean?" Her younger sister sat up beside her.

"It's a place where people are abandoned. It's a place of abandonment!" The grandmother flung wide her arms and flopped backward onto the moss.

"I think I'm beginning to see."

Good gracious me and my tits! Where in mackerel did that story come from? I can't tell where Obāchan ends and I begin or if I made the whole thing up or if it was all Obāchan.

Mom never told any stories. No compound sentences for that woman, she thrived on subject verb object. But I guess I can't complain. She made my life easy and easy to assimilate if your grandmother is skinny enough to be stuffed in a closet. Not that she ever did and not that Obāchan would ever allow it. But in Mom's mind, the closet door never opened. Too bad, I say. Too bad about shit like that.

Naoe

The wind is warm and from the west, the ache melts from my toes. Chinook, I mutter, chinook. The winters are long here, and nothing like long winters to make you think and think. The days, grim and grit, and not even a soft persimmon to sweeten my day. Keiko is a Nutra-sweet woman and doesn't take any cream. She's an Ivory girl with eyebrows plucked and pencilled in darker. It's funny how children grow inside your body, but they turn out to be strangers. Funny how you can love someone but never learn to like them. And I'm no prize myself. Ahhh, old malformed Richard wasn't the only one whose winters stretched long and bitter. Old Shakespeare might have written a different play if there had been chinooks where he lived. A chinook does wonders to a body. My curled-in fingers slowly soften and I can bend them again. I carefully search in the folds of my clothes for the last moth hidden there, but it is too late. She falls, brittle and stiff to the floor by my feet. But the wind is warm and the crystals of ice that manage to whisper into the house slowly melt into puddles. Keiko comes to wipe them up and mops the entire floor as well.

"Move your feet, Obāchan," she says, and shoves the mop between the legs of my chair, between my slippered feet.

Wait, I say, I want to pick up my moth, but Keiko has already soaked her up in the strands of the mop. No matter, I say, never mind. There are eggs somewhere and there will be moths again. Ahh, it would be an easy thing to sleep now, to stop my mouth and close my eyes. But there are things still left to do.

There is a non-wind, in Japan, in the summer. When the air hangs thick. A breathless time of sucking air like water and Shige and I sat still, in the shade of the persimmon tree. If we moved, the air would stick to our skin like wet hot paper. So we sat motionless, like the stone gods, and watched sweat trickle down our faces. Only the cicadas had the will to stir.

After seven long years of burrowing beneath the soil,

seven long years of tender-white grub skin and wet dirt silence, they welcomed the heat with their newly brittled wings. They clung to the bark of trees and cried and shrilled in thrumming songs of ecstasy. The songs rippling outward on the sweat-moistened air around them.

"Naoe-chan, Shige-chan," Okāsan called. "I have cucumbers I cooled in the well. Come, eat. It will make you feel better."

We smiled to each other and slowly rose to our feet. We did not run like we did in the spring or autumn, but moved with languid arms and legs, as if we were stirring deep underwater.

Shige. What, you are seventy-five, eighty years old? And kind Fumiko, always smiling, even after the childless years. Still smiling, no doubt. Kiyokawa to end with us. You had no children, Shige. Fumiko. When you visited temples and climbed steep stairs to pray at the shrines, for a child. Send us a child, we will love any child, even if that child should be as small as the end of a finger. But to no avail. The gods didn't hear you, or perhaps they had other matters to tend to. And Keiko takes the name of her husband. Kiyokawa to end with me. Foolishness! To attach so much to the continuation of a name. You might have a grand name and still live and die as an idiot. What matters are the things you do, the things you say out loud.

Mukāshi, mukāshi, ōmukashi . . .

There lived a good couple who were married for many years. They were kindly people and loved each other dearly, but one unhappiness marred their life. They were not blessed with a child. So the couple prayed at the temple, every day, please bless our home with a child, even if that child were to be tiny, even if that child were to be the length of the tip of a finger. Their wish was granted and in due time, the woman gave birth to a tiny child, the length of the tip of her finger. They loved their son dearly, and called him Issun-Boshi.

Issun-Boshi grew up to be a brave and comely lad, even though he didn't grow in stature. One day, he expressed his wish to visit the capital. So his mother armed him with a needle from her sewing basket, gave him a bowl for a boat, and he drifted down the river, steering with a pair of chopsticks. When he arrived at the capital, he found work with a noble family and they were much pleased with his demeanour. Miwa, the daughter of the household, was particularly fond of him.

One day, Miwa decided to visit the temple to pray and Issun-Boshi accompanied her. As they walked through the dapple green of bamboo groves, two hideous *oni* jumped from the trees to accost the lovely girl. Issun-Boshi drew his needle and stabbed one of the *oni* in the toe.

"Itai! Itai!" he bellowed and looked down to see what had pricked him. When he saw tiny Issun-Boshi brandishing a sewing needle, he laughed and laughed until the ground shook. "My, what a fierce little warrior," he chuckled and picked up the brave lad between his thumb and forefinger.

"Unhand the maiden or you'll have me to deal with!" Issun-Boshi challenged, not the least intimidated by the strength and size of the monster.

"Why you mouthy little underfed manling! I'll eat you for a snack," the red *oni* laughed, and tossed him into his gullet. But the brave lad did not give up. He ran about the demon's great belly and stabbed his organs with his needle sword until the *oni* howled with pain and spewed him from his gut. The second *oni* bent low to pick him up, but Issun Boshi flew at the demon's eye and pierced the giant globe with his needle. The two howling *oni* fled from the great warrior, back to their mountain home. As they ran, one of the demons dropped a magical mallet. A mallet which could be swung, *ichi, ni, san,* and asked to grant any wish desired. The lovely daughter of the noble family saw what the monsters had dropped and picked it up with joy.

"Issun-Boshi! Now you can grow to the size of normal men and we can become married!" Miwa cried, her heart filled with love and admiration for her mighty little warrior.

"Let this be so," the youth answered, and Miwa swung the mallet, *ichi, ni, san,* and Issun-Boshi grew bigger and broader and, in fact, was a great samurai. The family were overjoyed when they heard the story and gladly agreed to their marriage. Issun-Boshi joined their family as an equal despite his modest past. But his sudden stature, his noble position and his victory over two *oni* filled the lad's heart with pride and his kindly demeanour became a thing of the past. When Miwa lay down to sleep beside her new husband, he cared not a whit for her pleasure, but tore into her in what he thought suited his manly position. Miwa wondered what had happened to the boy she had loved. She bled but did not cry.

Many weeks passed. Issun-Boshi, who had been brave but gentle when he was so much smaller, became more arrogant and violent. Miwa waited and waited to see if Issun-Boshi was only going through a period of adjustment. When his kindly parents in their coarse cotton clothes came searching for their tiny son, he laughed at their poor appearance.

"I have no time for peasant talk," he mocked. "And if your tale is really true, than your son must have surely drowned in the river, for no such boy was ever heard of in the capital." Issun-Boshi's parents left, with tears of sorrow in their eyes, for the son they had lost. Miwa, who had been watching through a crack in the screen, felt her chest heave with hate.

That night, when Issun-Boshi had done with his wife, he lay snoring on his *futon.* Miwa crept softly to the family treasury and found the magical mallet. She softly slid back to where her husband lay, and swung, *ichi, ni, san,* Issun-Boshi shrinking shrinking, until he was the size of the tip of a finger. "Hey!" he squeaked, "hey, what are you—" Miwa lifted her graceful foot and crushed him beneath her heel. All that was left was a tiny stain on an otherwise spotless *tatami.*

Funny thing, Murasaki, how these stories keep changing. But that's the nature of all matter, I suppose. Can't expect the words to come out the same each time my tongue moves to speak. If my tongue were cut from my face, I would surely grow another. No, it is the nature of matter to change, and I feel the change coming from deep within my bones. Time ripens like a fruit and I must hurry, hurry.

I am used to hearing this roaring in my ears, the whistling scritch of dust pitting the walls. If the wind should stop, would I miss it, I wonder. Would my mouth crinkle up and my body fall to dust? There are ages of silence and ages of roaring, but one more thing remains. When the words have run their course there comes a time of change. I cannot stay in this chair forever.

"How was your day, Grandma?"

I start. Didn't hear him come in, my, so late already.

"Kyō no kaze wa chotto hageshikatta yo. Chotto kotaeta ka na," I say, waiting for his always, "Glad to hear it." But he surprises me.

"I brought you something, Grandma. Thought you might like it."

It is a mushroom. Bigger, than my two fists held together and rich with the scent of soil. But this mushroom, somewhere, somehow, two spores must have melded together, because there is a huge bulge on the main body of the stem, a two-headed mushroom with two possible umbrellas filled with gills of tiny spores. I hold the mushroom in my crack-lined palms and breathe in deep, the smell of growing.

"Utsukushii," I sigh, look up to my daughter's husband. *"Arigatō."*

"Glad you like it," he says and wanders down the hallway to the shower. When he is gone, I raise the mushroom to my mouth to take a giant bite. The flesh so firm, so juicy. I munch and munch.

Useless to waste time on sentimental memory. I may be an old fool, but stupidity is another matter. So important to remember, but say the words out loud. Don't wallow in pools of yesterday, I say. Don't drown in yesterday's tears. The wind in Alberta is harsh, but he is also constant. The wind will wear away at soil, paint, skin, but he will never blow with guile.

There is a wind in Japan, called *kama itachi.* Scythe weasel.

We walked along the red dirt road, not even a breeze,

between long rows of tea. Okāsan held my hand and I sang songs I learned at school.

"You will be good, child?"

"Hai, Okāsan, I will be very good."

"You will work hard and listen to the elders and not ask silly questions?"

"Hai, Okāsan. I will work very hard and bring home lots of money so we can have nice things again and lots and lots of food." Okāsan only held my hand tight and said nothing more. We walked down the road, the tea so green beside us. Cicadas thrummed and shrieked. Their cries were the only movement in the dust we raised with our feet.

Sudden sting/slash razor cutting across the backs of my legs I screamed. No sound, no whisper, nothing, but it returns whip-like through still air, even cicadas silent, and slashes across my chest, my *kimono* in tatters, the skin parted. Blood. So sudden and gone and I stood howling in the middle of the road, bleeding, Okāsan looking frightened holding me close. Searching with her eyes for someone, something, who cut me up, but there is nothing there. Nothing.

"What was it Okāsan? Who hurt me?" I sobbed, and clung to my solid mother.

"It was the *kama itachi.* An evil wind that moves with the speed of a weasel and cuts with the sting of a scythe."

"But why, why did he hurt me? I wasn't bad," I said, tears drying in my mother's *kimono.*

"He marked you, child. Naoe-chan, your life will be a difficult one. And you must always be strong. Come, we must leave this evil place." Okāsan picked me up, even though I was too big to be carried, and hurried from that road. I tucked my thumb in my mouth, for there was no one there to see me. I looked back over Okāsan's shoulder, and thought I saw something streak beneath the long dark rows of tea.

There are ages of silence and ages of roaring, but these too must come to a close. The full-bellied moon hangs low in the sky and I feel a stirring in my bones. In the hollows of my mouth. It is a time of change.

Ahhh, so easy to say, but another matter to open a door, step out, and close it behind me. Leaving what I know to explore what I don't. That takes more than just a simple wish or a passing thought. Easier yet just to stay put in my chair of incubation. I never claimed to be brave. *Che!* This snivelling doesn't become me, and the wind mocks my weakness. No. I cannot sit here forever. The prairie wind will dry me out, even as I sit, turning me into a living mummy. I'll be trapped for eternity uttering hollow sounds, words without substance. I would rather disembowel my innards then stay a prisoner of my own choice. Ritual *harakiri* so beautiful in theory but not so pretty when intestines spill like giant worms out of the body. The stink of digested food turning into shit. What a silly way to die, and no one ever talks about who gets to clean up the mess. Not to mention the actual pain of slicing open your own body.

There are things I haven't experienced yet. Moments of joy I haven't allowed myself to live. I don't want to die before I've ever fallen into my flesh or laughed myself silly. There are so many things I want to do and I'm ready to begin them now. Keiko and Murasaki need to grow without my noisy presence and I need to live outside the habit of my words. I go.

Of course, I will not leave empty-handed. There was a time when a person could travel with only a coat on her back and journey from place to place. Trade stories for a place to sleep, a bowl of rice or fish. But this time has passed and I can trade nothing for my stories now. I'll just fetch Keiko's purse, no, leave her Visa, she uses it so often, she'll miss it, surely. I'll take the MasterCard instead. And eighty dollars. She'll think Shinji took it. What else? Ah, so hard to leave, my body so used to the form of the chair. Foolishness! I must leave this chair like a husk, leave like a newly formed cicada. A silk moth. Twenty years is long enough. Only a fool will howl forever. No, I must truly leave. Keiko will worry, I suppose, for all that she pretends otherwise. But Murasaki, Murasaki will linger with me forever.

I leave you a letter, Keiko. If you choose, you may understand.

You dismantle our bed, taking the screws out of the headboard and along the frame. The mattress and the box are leaning against the wall. We lift the mattress out together, then the box, the headboard and the pieces of the frame. We load them up into the back of a U-Haul trailer which we pull behind your car.

"What brought this on, anyway?" I ask, driving slowly.

"I don't know. It just came to me suddenly. It was a—what do you call it? A brain wave!" you smile, pleased with your memory.

"Are you sure you can afford it? The bed's still perfectly fine, you know.

"I'm sure. Aren't you the one who says we should be more immediate? 'That we shouldn't let habit and complacency dictate the direction of our lives'?" you say, raising one eyebrow higher than the other.

"Che! Don't mimic me." I pull into the back alley behind the Salvation Army. Two women come out to help unload the bed and they thank us for our donation. We drive to Kensington to a futon shop. And I feel excitement tickling against my chest.

"What's your biggest futon?" you ask, hands resting on your hips.

"That would be the Shōgun size!" a sales clerk says, rubbing his hands together.

"We'll take it," you say, then turn to me. "What colour do you want?"

"Purple," I breathe.

PART TWO

She bundled herself in the thickest coat she could find, wrapped one scarf around her neck and one around her head. Tied the ends beneath her chin. She opened the snap of the purse on the kitchen table and flipped through the wallet. Pulled the bills out and counted them once, twice, then pocketed some, returned the rest. She chose a credit card and peered carefully. It was much too dark to make out the lines and swirls of the signature, so she flicked the kitchen light on and the sudden glare made her squint. The bright light was as loud as sound in the quiet of a midnight kitchen. She looked upward, at the the ceiling, but there were no floorboard creaks so she sat at the table and practiced forging the signature on a paper towel. When she was finally satisfied, she tore the towel into shreds and burned them in the sink. Tucked the card into a deep pocket with the cash.

She turned to the fridge and opened the door, perusing the contents with her lips pursed, a finger tapping her cheek. She muttered as she chose a wedge of cheese, a pomegranate, pita bread, nasty tasteless thing but it was light and it would keep, an apple, a package of Burns weiners, did she have no pride? Ah, but travellers can't be choosers, a Sunkist orange, was there nothing Japanese in the fridge at all? Not one single thing? And way at the back, behind pickled herring gone cloudy and mystery jars of no discernable origins, she found a tiny crock of salted seaweed. She snatched it up and slowly twisted the lid open, took a tentative sniff. Salt and sea. It was fine. She dipped a wrinkled pinkie into the black paste and sucked it from her finger in appreciative smacks. Smack! Smack! She twisted the lid back on and set the jar on the growing mound of food cluttered at her feet. A six-pack of beer. Much too heavy but it would go so nicely with the seaweed paste and the salted squid she'd saved up. She sighed. And added the beer to her stores. She looked down at the collection and shut the fridge door reluctantly.

There was enough food to be heavy, but not enough to last. She would have to hitch a ride as often as she could. She reached into her *monpe* pocket and took out a neatly folded *furoshiki*. She shook it out with a snap of her wrist so that the square piece of cloth was flat on the floor. Arranged the food on top of the *furoshiki*, distributing the weight evenly, then tied two diagonal corners in the center of the square. Tied the remaining two corners over top of the first knot. The sea paste she kept in her pocket with the money and salted squid. She hefted the weight of the *furoshiki* and glanced around the kitchen. Turned off the light. Black. Stood still in the darkness until her eyes adjusted, a bent and huddled figure.

As she walked down the hall, she stretched out brittle fingers to stroke the chair she had sat in for more years than she could hold in the cup of her hands. The straight wooden back, no cushion or armrests for comfort. She was drawn to it through force of habit, drawn by the patterns in her body.

Was tempted to sit once more, inside the soft curve of the seat that her bony buttocks had carved over two decades, but no! The chair had lent her stability in the midst of prairie dust and wind, but she could easily let it become her prison. She set her lips. Rubbed a hand over her eyes and brow, her back bent, her bundle of food at her feet. She whispered *ja ne*, with something close to loss or memory. The old woman stroked the back of the chair with a steady hand, then picked up her *furoshiki*. Opened the door.

The wind almost snatched the door from her hand in a blast of ice and dust, but she hung on tightly. Couldn't let the door slam before she even had a chance to take one step outside. Held tight, walked over the threshold into the swirl of snow outside. She closed the door behind her.

• • •

Naoe

Snow! It would have to snow the night I choose to leave. Ha! Blow on, blow on, Woman of the Snow. *Yuki-Onna*. Funny how I hated the wind so, when I was sheltered from it. We are sisters, you and I, and your cool breath upon my cheeks will comfort me. Ahhh, this air is sweet and the crystals of ice in my hair shiver like tiny cymbals. It is good to leave. Good to leave that house of dusty words. Too easy to sit and talk and talk when I can walk and talk instead. Ah, fool. March on.

Gawa gawa gawa gawa
Ototatete
Are are morino mukōkara
Soro soro detekuru hikōsen.

But wait. I should. I want to see before I leave this place forever. The *fushigi* smell where the mushrooms are growing. Here, so near. I would like to dip my fingers in the moist soil where they ripen in the dark. Turn back, woman, turn back. There are no pillars of salt in my culture. I will see before I leave. *Mattaku!* This *furoshiki* is going to get heavy. It's heavy enough already, no telling how heavy it'll be when I've walked a league or two, however far that may be. I'll find someone to give me a ride, once I'm on the highway.

Yuki-Onna. Woman of the Snow. Locked in your story of beauty and death. Let me release you. Press your icy lips to mine, there, and death will flee from my mouth of fresh ginger. I am old, but I'm still full of brine and *sake.* There, much better, I say and what? Your cheeks become rosy. Here, sit a while, enough of that hovering on wind. A body could get dizzy, watching you whisk around so. The snow is soft and you must be tired, all those years trapped in a story not of your creation. Are you thirsty? I have beer. It'll ease your thirst and thicken your blood. No? Why I've just the thing for a pale woman like you. Here, take. Why it's a pomegranate, child. No, of course you've never seen one, they would never grow in the snow. Beneath the leather skin, there are droplets of ruby so sweet you'll never taste the bitter dust of death again. Let me break it in half. Take them, child. Sink your teeth into the fruit. Suck. Yes, I know. You stay and rest, but I must be going to see some mushrooms.

So much snow blowing, I really can't see, but I must be getting closer. I can smell the sour compost. It hangs like a ripe wet cloth above the compost barn. I like this sound, this squeak squeak of snow beneath my boots. Everything filled with sound and story. Why a body could get lost with all this noise, but the nose never lies. Sniff. Sniff. Actually, you can taste with your nose if you're really sensitive. Like a dog, or maybe a snake. No, that's not quite right. A snake tastes smells on his tongue? Or he smells tongues on his taste. Or smells taste on his tongue—but I babble and scrabble—snakes are dreaming of sun-warmed rocks and dogs are twitching their toes in rabbit delight, but this old woman must walk!

• • •

She walked with an easy pace, face thrust into the bite of wind, hands clasped behind her back, holding her bundle of supplies. She didn't stop at the compost barn, but trudged on farther to the second building. Stood outside a small door for a moment, then opened it. She stepped inside.

And bathed in a blanket of soil and moisture. She stood still in the darkness, blinking in wonder. Surprised when she felt a warm wetness trickling down her cheeks. Pulled the gloves off her hands with clumsy fingers and reached to touch her face. When she held her fingers before her eyes, they glowed with phosphorescent beauty. She smiled. The old woman could smell the lingering brown aroma of coffee and the under-smell of formaldehyde. The cakey yeasty sugar smell of old Twinkie wrappers. So black, so dark, she could only see with her nose, with the surface of her senses. She felt a soft nudging at her boots, and felt a warm hump at her feet. Heard a blink of eyes. The fast thump thump thump of tail beating the floor. She crouched down to let the dog smell her hands, to lick her cheek and brow. The woman scratched tender dog ears and belly, then reached inside her pocket to tear off some dried squid legs. She ran her hands along the wall until she found an open doorway and left the coffee room to the sounds of jaws chewing a welcome midnight snack.

The hallway was huge, like the wet cavern of a whale. Her eyes adjusted slowly, and she could only see varying shades of black. Could feel the empty space around her. Could almost hear the fungus hum of mushrooms growing behind closed doors. The density of moisture clung heavily to her clothes. It was much warmer than the house she had lived in, and she unbuttoned her heavy coat and shrugged it off. Unwrapped her scarves and dropped them. Tugged her sweater over her head and pulled down her polyester *monpe* with both thumbs, taking her panties down with them, and stepped out of her winter boots, socks still inside. She stood, shoulders slightly stooped, arms dangling, her pelvis thrust forward in weak posture. She looked like an aged shrimp in silent contemplation. But for the first time in decades, moisture filtered into her body. Moisture rich with peat moss and fungal breath. Slowly seeping into parchment, osmosis of skin and hair. The blanket wet of humidity enclosing her tiny figure. Her sallow cheeks shone a little more roundly and the loose skin where she once had breasts began to rise like bread, like *mantō*. Her skin, so dry, slowly filled, cell by cell, like a starving plant, the mushroom moisture filling her hollow body. The wet tinkling into her brittleness. Blood stirring, restless. Like silk threads, they wound through her. Old chicken arms grew longer, filling with supple strength, her buttocks curving, swelling, with flesh and longing. She could hear her body filling, the rippling murmur of muscles and bones, squeak of hair growing long and smooth, long enough to sweep the soft skin of her back. Her yellow parchment skin growing taut, glowing coolly like newborn silkworms. She ran her palms from her collarbones over breasts belly hips thighs. Laughed aloud in wonder. Stood tall and straight and stretched on her toes, flung her hands skyward.

She strode down the dim hallway, the floor shaking beneath her feet. The buckets on hooks against the walls clattered with each step she took and some fell, rolled under her feet to be squashed like Styrofoam cups. She breathed in great draughts and followed the scent ripe with fungal ecstasy. She stood before a door marked Number 9. Stretched out a hand and pushed it inward on noiseless hinges. Heard the timeless murmur of mushrooms hush. She had to bend low, tuck her head into her chest and enter sideways to fit her giant body through the frame of the door. And finally she stood among them.

Vast rows upon rows, beds of peat and darkly, richly wet. And mushrooms. Such mushrooms. They gleamed like newly hatched silk-worms, like jellyfish and oysters. The only sound the drip drip of moisture condensed on the ceiling, plipping into tiny puddles on the damp cement floor. Welcome, welcome, into this world of moist. She walked between the longs rows of beds, through puddles warm as blood and stood naked in the centre of the room. The fungal silence as thick as the moisture around her. And she lay down, spread her arms, her legs wide and peat water soaking, lay down, in puddles warm and glowing. Closed her eyes, feeling the seeping the sinking into. Slipped deeper, and deeper, her eyes closed, her hands floating on the water. Floating towards herself. Followed the bones of her ribs to curving flesh. She stroked her breasts, the soft skin of her nipples, pinched gently the skin puckering with sudden ache. Touched her own breasts as she would if they were another's. Cupped them in her palms and held them like two hearts. Her legs stirred in the peaty water, the rich scent headier than any musk, any perfume. The soft wet mud kisses on her cheek, inner arms, the skin beneath her knees. Along her inner thighs. She left brown fingers of peat etched on her breasts. Her hands smoothed down, down, swell of belly, curving to her pleasure. Softly, softly, her hands, her fingers, the moisture, her ache, peat warm as blood, the moisture seeping into hair, skin, parchment softening elastic stretch of muscles gleaming a filament of light. Murmur murmur forming humming earth tipping under body swelling growing resound and the SLAM of breath knocked from lungs, beyond the painful register of human sound, the unheard chorus of mushrooms.

• • •

We lie on our giant futon, so big that it covers completely the floor of your bedroom. It is a decadent pleasure. There is no frame beneath us, just the futon, and our naked bodies on top. We move in our sleep, all over the expanse of the floor, then meet each other in surprise when we wake up.

You are asleep. You were tired and couldn't stay awake. But the stories, true or not, are waiting to be told. I cannot hold them until you are ready to hear them, so I keep on saying the words out loud and you nod, your eyelids flicker in your sleep. Trust me.

Here's a true story . . .

Murasaki

Local Elderly Woman Disappears
Search Continues

Late Tuesday night, the immigrant mother-in-law of local mushroom farmer, Sam Tonkatsu went missing during blizzard-like snow conditions.

"We're very worried," says Sam's wife. "We just want her to come home."

Local RCMP and neighboring ranchers are combing the countryside, but weather conditions hinder their search.

"Cases like this are difficult," says Constable Norton. "An elderly woman isn't likely to survive a single night during weather like we've been experiencing."

What is surprising is that most town folk were unaware that the old woman was even living with the Tonkatsus.

Foul play has been ruled out.

"What happened to your grandma?"

"She went back to Japan. She got sick of all this snow and dust and up and left. I don't blame her."

"What happened to your grandma?"

"She went ape-shit and was raving, frothing at the mouth and she ran naked from the house screaming like the pagan she is."

"What happened to your grandma?"

"She started to grow fur all over her body and at first, we thought it was a symptom of illness or something like she wasn't eating enough so her body was compensating with fur to keep her warm but we found out she was actually a *tanuki* who had assumed the form of a woman so she could marry my grandfather because he had set her free from a trap and she wanted to thank him by becoming his wife, but now, she wanted to return to the wilds whence she came."

I found out then, that everybody, including me, was always looking for a story. That the story could be anything. They would eat it.

"What happened to your Obāchan?" he asked, touching my hair, my face, just so.

"I don't know," I said. "I won't know until she leaves again."

"How can she leave again if she's already gone?"

"She can leave again with me."

He didn't say anything. Just touched my hair, my face. Just so.

Mind you, the story can be anything, but there have to be details. People love details. The stranger, the more exotic, the better. "Oooooh," they say. "Aaaaaaah." Nothing like a freak show to make you feel normal, safe by comparison. "Tell us about the feet," they say. "Did your grandmother have to bind her feet when she was little?" Actually, feet were never bound in Japan, but someone keeps on perpetuating this myth. It always goes back to that. The binding of the feet. Deformities. Ritual Hari Kari. Actually, it's *harakiri* but go on saying Hairy Carrie for all I care. It's not about being bitter. You're invited somewhere to be a guest speaker. To give a keynote address. Whatever that is. Everybody in suits and ties and designer dresses. You're the only coloured person there who is not serving food. It's not about being bitter. You just notice. People talk race this ethnic that. It's easy to be theoretical if the words are coming from a face that has little or no pigmentation. If your name is Hank and you have three blond kids, no one will come up to you in the Safeway produce section and point at a vegetable and ask, "What is that?"

I was standing in the ethnicChinesericenoodleTofupattiesexotic vegetable section of Safeway. Fingering, squeezing stroking Japanese eggplants for firmness, taut shiny purple skin and no rust spots. I love shopping. The touching of vegetables. Lingering of fruits and tap tapping my fingers on watermelon husks. Just minding my business and choosing eggplants.

"What is that, exactly? I've always wondered."

I looked up from my reverie and a face peered down on me. A kindly face. An interested face.

"It's an eggplant."

"Oh really!" Surprisewonderjoy. "How wonderful! This is what *our* eggplants look like. They're so different!" She held up a round almost-black solid eggplant. Bitter skin and all. She looked up at the handmade signs above the vegetables with the prices marked in dollars per pound.

LOO BOK $.89/lb they read BOK CHOY $.49/lb SUEY CHOY $.69/lb

"What are they called in *your* language?"

I looked up at the signs.

"I don't speak Chinese," I said.

"Oh. I'm sorry."

Sorry for what? I wondered. And there, right above the eggplants where all the other handwritten signs were:

I took the long and graceful eggplant I still held in my hand and smacked it smartly against the sign.

"Here. Here it is," I said. And turned my back to examine *hakusai* leaves. Suey Choy in Chinese according to the Safeway produce staff. Leave me in peace. Let a woman choose her vegetables in peace. Vegetable politics.

Mom never bought eggplants when she went shopping. Not even the hugely round black Canadian kind. Who knows where they come from. She didn't buy *hakusai* or *shōga* or *shiitake* or *daikon* or *satoimo* or *moyashi* or *nira*. There was a vegetable blind spot in her chosen menu and Obāchan must have felt it sorely. I only noticed what I was missing after I began to question. When I was in a position to miss something I never knew I had missed. But there was one thing Mom could forgive and that was a box of Jap oranges for Christmas. Funny how they're called Jap oranges. When they are technically called Mandarin oranges and Mandarin isn't even a place but a Chinese language. Funny how words and meaning twist beyond the dimensions of logic. Mom wasn't very logical either. She thought if the church could buy Christmas oranges, then she might make this one allowance and I wouldn't be contaminated. I couldn't get enough. I hunkered beneath our twinkle tree and alternately wolfed them down or sucked like a thirsty man after crossing a desert of mashed potato. I ate so many at once that my skin started changing colour. Funny thing. If you eat too many Jap oranges, your skin turns yellow.

I was lying beneath the absurd lights flicker flacker and sweet tang of pine sap, an empty Mandarin orange box and green tissue squares all around me. I was replete. I looked it up in the dictionary and that's exactly how I felt. I raised my fingers to my nose and citric sour smell of peel. I sniffed again. Held my hands above my head and looked at the twinkle tree between my fingers. And I noticed it. Funny, I thought, my hands look yellow. Maybe it's the Christmas lights. Pulled my hands up close and stared. No, they were definitely yellow. Turning brighter by the minute and spreading down my arms. I laughed out loud.

"Look Mom!" I yelled. Just as excited as the time I had red shit from eating too many beets. "Lookit my hands!"

Mom turned from the sink, pushed her glasses up her nose a bit and peered down on my palms.

"Oh God," an invocation as opposed to a curse. "Oh my God." She grabbed my wrists and dragged me to the sink.

"Ouch!" I said, tugging back. "Ouch, don't! It's only the oranges. I ate the whole box, that's all."

She turned the hot water on full blast. Dumped Sunlight on my hands and started scrubbing with an SOS pad.

"Ow!" I screamed. "Don't Mom! It's only the oranges! It's only the oranges!"

"Yellow," she was muttering, not even hearing me. "Yellow, she's turningyellow she'sturningyellow she's—"

Obāchan, whose voice was constant as the prairie wind, who hadn't stopped muttering, singing, humming, yelling for as long as I could ever remember. Who never stopped voicing her very existence. That was the only time Obāchan ever stopped her refrain. The only time that sound stopped pouring from her mouth. The sudden silence after fourteen years of torrential words hit Mom over the head like a concrete block. She dropped my hands and muttered something about a headache and went upstairs to lie down and didn't get up again for three days. Like Christ. I rinsed my tender hands in cool water. Walked down the hall to Obāchan's chair. I crawled into her lap, even though my elbows and knees spilled every which way, and snuggled my head into her skinny neck. Obāchan started her soothing refrain again.

It's funny how you can sift your memories, braid them with other stories. Come up with a single strand and call it truth.

Of course everything wasn't hunky dory between my Obāchan and me. It's easy to be romantic when she has been gone for over ten years and you live in a split-level bungalow in north west Calgary. When you deliver newspapers in the middle of the night, volunteer for the Committee Against Racism and sleep long and warm during the brightness of the day. Of course there was tension because she lived with us in Nanton and couldn't keep her mouth shut. Of course there were times when I was acutely embarrassed. Of course.

"What's your grandma saying?" Patricia asked, when she stepped inside our door for the first time. Obāchan was patting her on the head like a puppy and chatting away. We had been assigned out-of-town pals in school for when blizzards made the roads too dangerous to travel. The pals got to stay over night in town until the weather calmed down enough for them to get home.

"Uhhmm," I thought frantically. Patricia was the most popular girl in class and I desperately wanted to be her best friend. "She says she's really happy to meet you and she hopes we can be good and kind friends with each other and uhhmmm, she likes your hair like that and uhhhmmmm, maybe we ought to play outside until supper."

"But it's blizzarding outside," Patricia said, smiling.

"Uh, yeah. I guess she must be joking. Ha ha."

Mom had left us Oreos for a snack, and we gulped cold milk to wash down the cookie mud. It was freezing inside the house and Obāchan was yelling to drown out the wind. Her chair creaking beneath the force of her voice. Patricia didn't say anything, but she kept looking at me when she thought I wouldn't notice. Kept glancing at Obāchan who didn't move from her chair. We sat down to watch "The Flintstones" but the howling wind, my noisy Obāchan, the snow snaking around our ankles made it all impossible.

"Do you want to explore the mushroom farm?" I asked.

"Yeah! That'd be neat."

We bundled up with snow clothes, still wet and icy. I leaned over to give Obāchan a peck on the cheek, and she nodded, but didn't stop her voice from challenging the blizzard wind. Wrapped itchy cold scarves around our heads so that only our eyes peeped out. And stepped outside into a blast of ice pellets.

We trudged to the mushroom farm, the west wind blowing knives into our backs, snaking around to fling daggers from the north. A heavy moisture steam surrounded the two buildings. They were shrouded with mist that no amount of wind could whisk away.

"They look like enchanted castles!" Patricia yelled above the slice of wind.

"Yeah," I yelled back, then muttered beneath my breath, "or a penitentiary."

"What's in this building?" Patricia pointed to the first barn.

"That's just the compost building. It stinks in there.

And it'll get into your clothes. The growing barn is better. There's more to see," I panted. The wind was snatching my air away before I had time to gulp it.

"All right. Let's go in. I'm freezing!"

We tried to open the little side door, the bottom of it raised two feet off the ground, but it was frozen shut. We took turns kicking until it burst in and we both tried to squeeze through at the same time. Laughing, screeching, we tumbled inside and fell into a heap. I kicked the door shut from where we were lying, still giggling uncontrollably.

"What are you doing, girl?"

I nearly fell out of my skin and Patricia gave a little gasp. Joe had been standing there the whole time, but we hadn't seen him in the dim light.

"Nothing," I scowled.

"You coming to pick? Your friend too?"

"No. I'm just showing Patricia the mushroom farm. No one said anything about working. We came to play here, because it's too cold to play outside."

"Ohhh?" Joe said, in his annoying way. "You want to make boxes?"

"No! We don't want to make boxes!" I yelled, and grabbed Patricia's hand and we fled down the huge cavernous hall, our feet ringing echoes on the sheets of metal covering the drainage ditch.

"Who was that?" Patricia whispered. We had made it to the coffee room and there were cake donuts left over from the three o'clock break. We realised that we were soaking wet from moisture and sweat. The humidity inside kept the warmth right next to our skin, and we couldn't undress fast enough. Kicked heavy moonboots off our heels and tore snow pants off our legs. Flung our scarves from our faces and left our jackets lying where they fell.

"That was Joe," I scoffed, showing off. "He's our manager. But he doesn't boss me around."

We poured ourselves coffee and dumped three lumps of sugar and three spoonfuls of Coffeemate into our Styrofoam cups. Ate the donuts.

"He's kinda cute!" Patricia giggled. I was shocked and embarrassed at the same time.

"Joe?! You've got to be kidding? He's like forty or something. He's a boat person!" Like that would explain everything.

"I still think he's kinda cute," Patricia said, confused at my denial. "You're Japanese, but I still think you're pretty too."

"Thanks," I said. Confused, myself, for what I didn't know. "Let's go exploring."

We left the break room in short sleeved T-shirts and my mushroom picking runners I kept at the farm. Our tummies sloshing with weak, sweet coffee. I showed Patricia a room where the mushrooms were growing. In the silent hum of wet darkness, the mushrooms glowed like cave fish.

"Wow," she whispered. Like in church. "Wow. I thought you grew mushrooms in the fields or something. Or inside a greenhouse. Not like this."

We stood in the front of the room, listening to moisture condense on the walls, then slowly stream downward. Patricia mesmerized, and I was wondering why I had never noticed Joe's looks before. There was the clang cling of buckets and the pickers filed into the room.

"Oh! Murio! Are you picking?" Jane asked. She was the head picker, and Joe's wife.

"No," I sighed. "I'm just showing my friend the farm."

"Oh, that's nice. Nice to meet you. I'm Jane, Joe's wife," she said, and held out her mushroom stained hand. Her fingers caked with mushroom skin.

Patricia held out her hand and shook.

"Pleased to meet you. I'm Patricia. I think Joe is very handsome!" Patricia giggled, and Jane giggled with her, turning bright red with pride and embarrassment.

"Yes, I think so too," she giggled and yelled out in Vietnamese so everyone could know. The women stopped picking to laugh and laugh, tears dropping from their eyes. Patricia laughed with them and I stood watching from outside the small circular glow of Jane's mushroom-picking light.

"Nice friend," Jane said, patting my arm. "Maybe you won't be so lonely now."

"Yeah," I said, "yeah, I hope so." I felt so funny that I had to do something with my hands. I just couldn't play while everyone worked around me, so Patricia and I made cardboard boxes and stacked them ten high until Mom phoned from the house to tell us to come back for supper.

"Making boxes isn't so bad," Patricia yelled above the howling of the wind. "Lots better than slopping pigs and cleaning out their shit. Race ya!"

We stumbled, plodded, through drifts of snow in our heavy moonboots. Laughing icy knives into our lungs. As we came closer to the house, I could smell a special occasion ham burning in the oven.

I felt for Mom too, you know. Don't get me wrong. You couldn't have a bridge party if you had an immigrant mother who sat muttering beside the door. Who waited for people to enter so she could spit foreign words at them. She would stare people in the eyes and never turn away or blink. It made it impossible for the macaroons to go down the throat. And a prayer meeting would turn into an exorcism if Obāchan started howling back at the wind. So Mom made her choices and she lived with the consequences. She always talked about Silver Springs but she never packed Obāchan's things. And she always washed Obāchan's hair. Mom isn't the wicked mother figure in the Walt Disney cast of good guys and bad guys. It was another thing of parent/child conflict. Add a layer of cultural displacement and the tragedy is complete.

That's a lie. One of many, I suppose. Mom is a whole different story and one I can't even begin to comprehend. Me sitting here and Mom sitting there and Obāchan out and about but hovering around my ears. Obāchan away when my words are born so I'm responsible for the things I utter. Better than being utterless. I learn slowly.

Funny how memory is so selective. How imagination tags along and you don't know where something blurs beyond truth. If I said I was telling the truth, would anyone believe me? Obāchan would, of course. The truth of anything at that particular moment. What more could you ask for?

I was always hungry for words, even when I was very little. Dad, the man without an opinion, and Mom hiding behind an adopted language. It was no wonder I was so confused, language a strange companion. I never knew what I should do. If I should tie it up then ignore it, or if I should mould and shape. Manipulate language like everyone else around me. I never understood the words she said, but I watched and learned. And I begin my understanding now. Obāchan took another route, something more harmonious. Showed me that words take form and live and breathe among us. Language a living beast.

I'm not saying that the only sound in our home was the sound of Obāchan's voice. There were times when we sat at the dinner table, when she went upstairs to get away from the smell of boiled beef. We'd talk then, Mom and I, and sometimes Dad would offer a word or two. It's just that the things we talked about would never have the power to linger. "How was school?" and, "Pass the gravy boat," were sad substitutes for my malnourished culture. But how to ask the questions if you don't have the vocabulary to express them?

There were words in excessiveness when we sat in church. All those "Thous" and "Thees" and "manifestation," now there's a doozie for you! I even knew when I was little that their words were falsely weighted. That god was not a bellower, but light as motes of dust. That there wasn't a definitive god but god-spirits living in everything I saw around me. In the wind, the snow, the soft earthly curves of the prairies stretching ever eastward. The sound of crickets thrumming, the whistles of gophers in the warmish spring and the shrieks of redtails, swirling high above me. The gods would never linger in pews stinking with selfish guilt. With all those wads of gum.

When Pastor Lysol was appointed to Mom's church, he brought with him a whole new agenda. There was a Women's Health League, what would he know about it? Men in the eighties, no shit, unfortunately. Seniors for Saving and what I called Spill Yer Guts, my personal favourite. After the very young were sent downstairs to play with felt, Pastor Lysol would call on anyone to share.

"If during the past week, you have felt the hand of God

touch your lives, please share with us, your family together in Christ. Come, there is no need to feel self-conscious. Your pain is our pain. Your joys, our joys. If there is anything you would like to say. Nothing is so shameful that God will not forgive. If you have sinned, come, confront your sin and, we, your brothers and sisters in the Lord, will share with you all our love. Come forward. Have no fear."

He held his palms outward, in the posture a lot of people paint Jesus in. Spoke with a gentle voice, like a lamb with honey in it's mouth. And everyone waited. That nervous sour anticipatory stink of people waiting to hear of sin. Degradation. Vicarious thrill of ooooh and aaaaah. Everyone shifted anxiously in their seats, turning around, glance here and there to see who would stand up. Spill their guts. It always made me feel quiggly in my stomach. How adults got their thrills in such strange and unnatural ways. But it didn't stop me from turning my head around, waiting to see who would talk.

"I—"

All the heads swung around to the left, the far back of the room. It was Pastor Lysol's wife! There was a murmur murmur then a sudden stillness.

"I—I——"

Everyone craned their heads, willing her to continue.

"Yes," Pastor Lysol said kindly, like he thought Jesus would have. "Yes, don't be afraid."

"I have c-commited s-sins of the flesh!" she gasped. An intake of breath by the whole congregation sucked all the oxygen from the room and everyone started to pant softly. "I have felt the Devil tempting me. He c-comes to m-me when I am at my weakest and—and—"

"Have no fear. We are not here to judge, but to lead you

in the ways of the Lord. We are your family and our love knows no boundaries. Speak, woman, and find peace with the Lord," the pastor said kindly, like he was talking to a stranger and not his wife.

"The Devil makes me touch myself!" she spat out like a chunk of cancer. Good lord! I thought. Good lord! She doesn't need the church. She needs to listen to Doctor Ruth. Sex therapist extraordinaire and make sure you use a condom. Good lord!

"The Devil makes me feel so good, I can't stop. He whispers in my ear, 'If it feels good, it can't be a sin, can it? Go on, it's okay. Just do it.' And I do! I do!" she wept. Everyone clucked their tongues in pity but some women were squirming in their seats with I don't know what. A few people started to clap, but it petered out as it became apparent that it wasn't quite the right time for it. The pastor's wife's sobs quieting down and she started hiccuping, wiping mucous from her nose.

"Oh Lord!" cried out Pastor Lysol. "Oh Lord, hear the words of Thine weak children! Have pity on these, Thy children of flesh, so susceptible to the call of their flesh. Our puny existence so moiled with transgressions we cannot hear the higher calling. Forgive the weakness of women. So little they have changed since the fall of Eve into earthly Sin. We can only turn to Thine eternal love and beg for forgiveness. Lord Father, please forgive that woman, and give her the strength to reach the purity of thought only found through Thine words. We beg of You. In Jesus' name. A-men."

The pastor's wife glowed with the prayer she had earned and everyone appreciatively licked their lips. After the service was over, the leaders from the Women's Health

League circled around the pastor's wife and congratulated her on her courage. There was a lot of talk during the fellowship potluck that day. People stood around with their plates of raisin-turds-and-carrot-shavings encased in lime Jell-O dessert. They waved their plastic forks around and argued over how many points the pastor's wife should receive for her performance.

At least Mom never joined that spectacle. I can thank the gods, not Greek, for that.

There are a lot of sad immigrant stories. Here's another one.

The Herald Funny True Stories Contest
Second Prize Winner, Miss Janet Duncan

I'm an elementary teacher in south west Calgary. There are many children from different cultures in my class and I find myself learning so much from them. It's a pleasure to teach and learn together.

This spring, there was a lovely new boy who had immigrated from Japan, with his family. His father was transferred to work in the Calgary office of Sanyo. Little Kenji, Ken, we call him, was quite shy, but he was really clever in mathematics. He learned very quickly, and his English skills were getting better and better all the time.

Well, we have show and tell at the beginning of each class, and Ken had declined from participating for several weeks. Then one day, he said he would like bring something to share with his friends.

Well, I was so pleased! I couldn't wait to see what kind of treasure he would show us. I was thinking perhaps a lovely fan or a silk kimono or something. I just couldn't wait.

Well, the next day arrives, and the bell has already rung and Ken is late. But I know he must be coming so I don't start the class, even though it is already 9:15. I finally hear Ken at the door, but there is an awful odour even before I have opened it. My eyes begin to water. Ken bursts open the door and the reek

> rolls in like a tidal wave! All the children scream "Ooooooh!" and scramble to the back of the class.
>
> Ken had brought a live skunk into the school!
>
> "Cat. My new cat." Ken was gulping. He must have been sprayed so badly that he couldn't smell any more. The full grown skunk was curled around his neck in fear of all the noise and his tail was sticking straight up and down. We were absolutely paralyzed and Ken didn't know what the commotion was all about and one enterprising young girl pulled the fire alarm. The children ran, screaming, outside and the whole school filed out. Ken came out with his skunk and the fire-men took it away in a net. My whole classroom had to be washed down with tomato juice.
>
> When I got home that day, I wrote a letter to the immigration office to suggest they offer wildlife identification courses as well as the English lessons.

Ba dum Bum

Sure I have some white friends. Some of my best friends are white.

Ba dum Bum

> "I must be a mushroom
> Everyone keeps me in the dark
> And feeds me horseshit"

Hyuck Hyuck. My boyfriend in junior high school bought that T-shirt for me on our three-week anniversary. All shiny decals, the slippery plastic kind that you sweat under when you are in direct sunlight. He was a cowboy. Still is, I suppose, heard he's a foreman out at Whiskey Coulee Ranch and riding bulls in the summer. Funny how you can spend a whole summer making out with someone and never really know or like him. All you remember is the very first time you ever felt the skin of a penis beneath your fingers. That particular odour.

Having to work all summer at the farm. At least it was cool inside. At least it was moist. I loved the prairie wind, but the scuttle dry heat of grasshopper wings, brittle as the days were long, wasn't a heat I loved. Even on my days off, when I knew it was my duty to lie in the sun and brown, slick with coconut-smelling oils, I didn't last. Julie and Patricia lying outside for hours on end, cucumbers on their eyes. They evenly toasted their pale bodies into a glowing red. I hated it. How the sun glared off the pages in my books so bright I got a headache, and the stink of coconut. Leaving greasy fingerprints on my precious books and having to go through the ordeal of sitting up every five minutes to peel back a strap, tug the cup of my bikini to see if the skin beneath was lighter. Having to wait for the crunch of gravel in the alley, of the boys walking by and seeing us in our splotchy splendour. I would sit beneath the crab apple tree, hugging its shrinking shadows. So busy reading, I would miss any boys that bothered to walk by.

I wasn't the only kid working at Dad's farm. At least not during the summer. In the summer, students would come by looking for a job and I wouldn't have to be the only kid working with all the adult regulars. Then, there'd be a couple of boys doing odd jobs. Maybe even get to learn how to drive the forklift if they were handy enough. A few girls would come out to pick mushrooms for some summer spending money, but they never lasted. The monotony, the dark, the tediously long hours. The strange trickling sound of Vietnamese conversation. So foreign and harsh to their ears, they couldn't bear to stay. All the regular pickers placed bets on how soon they would leave. The world record was two hours. They laughed. Funny how I picked with them for so many years, but I never learned a single word. I would just turn my ears inward and pluck at my own thoughts. Or think of nothing at all.

I was picking mushrooms at my own particular pace, flicking my knife to slice off the stems and plunk plunkplunk plunk of mushrooms dropping into my buckets. I almost dropped my knife and fell off the bed I was perched on when a sudden hand grabbed my ankle. I shrieked. The boys snickered.

"What do you want?! It's not three! You guys are supposed to be getting peat moss ready."

"Don't get your tit in a knot," Bob said, and snickered again.

"Yeah, keep your pants on," laughed Josh. "We just came to show you something."

"What? It better not be one of those dead pigeons." I hopped down from the third beds I was standing on and hunkered down with the boys. Josh held something in his hands, and at first it was too dark to figure out. I brought my light down. It was a salamander. I'd never seen one live before, never up close. All black and damp and moistly supple, the skin shiny tender of things that live in wet. I held out my hands.

"Let me hold it," my voice filled with wonder.

"Ahhh," Bob said, "aren't you even scared of it?"

"Why?"

"You're no fun at all," Josh complained. "Come on, let's go scare Joe."

"No!"

"Fuck off, Murry-O. We can do whatever we want."

"No. Give me that salamander."

They were surprised, and I was serious. Bob and Josh just shrugged their shoulders, embarrassed. Josh dangled the salamander by the tail and dropped it on my outstretched palm.

"All right, all right!" they said. "Relax already. Have the stupid thing," and backed out of the room, muttering "Women!" under their breaths.

"Where did you find it?" I yelled, as they left.

"In a bag of peat moss."

I peered down at the salamander cupped in the palm of my hands. How could it have been in the peat moss when the peat moss came from west of Edmonton? How would it get there in the first place? I'd never seen a salamander before, despite all my summers of tadpoles, frogs, and garter snakes. Gophers and crunchy black crickets too. Where did the creature come from? Displaced amphibian. The salamander turned its head slowly, this way and that, the light too close, too bright for it to see. I lifted my forefinger and gently, gently, touched its back. Stroked. The salamander was soft. I had thought it was slimy, with its moistly gleaming skin. But it wasn't. It was as soft as the skin on a penis.

"What are you doing, girl?" Joe asked.

I didn't even hear him come in. I just slowly raised my hands so he could see what I cupped in my palms so preciously. He tipped my hands just a little, so the light from my lamp shone more directly, on the glowing salamander.

"Mmmm," he said. "First time I see this in Canada."

"Me too."

"It's very far from home, huh."

"Yeah," I nodded, something dawning. "Yeah, I guess it is."

"There are salamanders in Japan too," you say, on the far corner of the futon. You are lying on your back with your two legs V-ing upwards against the corner walls.

I lie in the middle, on my belly. Flicking lint balls with my forefinger.

"We can go out, you know. We can do something else. This isn't a trap or anything," you say. "You can stop any time you want."

"No," I flip around so I'm not driven to flick lint balls. Stare upward at the long strand of dusty cobweb floating supplely from the ceiling. "I can't stop any time I want. But you can stop listening."

You sigh. Swing your feet down from the wall and roll into the middle of our futon. We cuddle together, our arms protecting each other. We huddle like thieves, like beggars. We huddle like lovers.

"No," you say, "I can't stop listening either."

Naoe

Wind toss sting slash of snow, too soft a word for something this cold, this sharp. But I'm warm up in my belly with three cans of beer and salt lick taste the corners of my mouth. Ahhh, nothing like seaweed paste to make a body thirsty! I could sit here awhile, chase snow pellets with my eyes, but *Chikishō!* I've sat too long. Long enough already! And who will see me in this ditch? A ride won't be offered if I'm not seen and which way should I choose to go? I could be going inside out for all I know, none of this natural instinct for direction. *Kekkō, kekkō!* At least my *furoshiki* is lighter now, I have that to thank. My life would be complete if I could smoke a cigarette. Twenty years between cigarettes is a little long. No matter! I'll walk and walk and the wind will serenade me. I'll walk and sing and laugh and shout. I'll scrape my heel into the black ice on the highway and inscribe my name across this country.

• • •

The woman trudged through the sting of ice crystals, leaning forward into the slice of the wind. Her hands were clasped behind her back and she walked with the slow steady pace of someone who plans to walk for a long time. Now and again, a semitrailer roared by in a swirl of dust and snow, buffeting her slender body. They either did not see her or chose not to. But she walked on, the snow squeaking beneath her boots, the wind howling about her ears. Beer, warm in her belly. The distance she travelled was meaningless in the vortex of ice and sound. She only set one foot in front of the other. Thought nothing of where, but turned outward her momentum to keep her surface warm. Steam rose from her body and billowed in a cloud around her. A pick-up truck caught her haunting figure in the glare of its high beams and braked slowly, slowly, red tail lights blinking, on the slick surface of the highway. It finally came to stop fifty yards ahead of her, and she jogged forward at the same time the truck started backing up. When she reached the cab of the truck, the door swung outward in a sweet scent of tobacco and horse sweat.

• • •

"Git'in, miss!"

Miss, no less! *Ara ma ha! ha! ha!*

"Musta froze right thru yer sense, walkin' 'bout on a night like this. Worryin' yer folks 'n such. T'aint my bizness, jist say so."

Mattaku! Konnani akarui hito to au no wa hisashiburi da ne!

"Froze thru ta yer tongue I reckon. No need ta talk I ain't no stranger ta silence, jist feelin' a bit chatty, bin drivin' nonstop fer a good stretch 'n need ta loosen my tongue a whiles not that I'm ulwez this way but I figger y'all walkin' by yerself might need ta be hearin' a friendly voice. Sher, everybudy gits caught up with loneliness 'n everybudy's got some sad tale hangin' 'roun ther sleeves but I figger ther's ulwez a loada sadness but that ulwez makes ya feel ixtra special when somethin' good comes by yer way 'n I guess I could offer ya smoke or somethin', ya born in Japan?"

"Yes and yes."

"I figger ya had the looka Japanese, 'n knew yer lookin' fer a butt, soon as ya got in the cab snuffin' up the smoke, here, have one."

I can't believe my eyes! He tosses a squished almost flat package of Mild Sevens! *Do yu koto daro?* I never believed in fate, so why should he present himself now, I wonder. And I am intrigued.

"Were you in Japan quite recently?" I ask.

"Yup."

"Was it nice?" Knowing that he just came from there made my heart twist with something I couldn't name. "I suppose your eyes would see it so differently. My Japanese eyes are at the back of my head, and they can only see backwards. My Japanese eyes are twenty years dimmed and I'm no fool. Who was that silly girl? Always clicking her heels, click click click, and wringing her hands so. Everyone knows that home is long gone and wishing won't make it otherwise. I was home only until I was five years old. I've been gone ever since. But tell me what you saw with your eyes. I am not so realistic that I can't listen with an eager ear."

"I dunno what I kin tell ya. I spint most my time roamin' the countryside, stayin' in *ryokans* 'n *minshukus.* People're kind in the country, not so hustle 'n bustle like Tokyo or Osaka. Little kids in ther school uniforms 'n little yellow packsacks would follow me 'roun 'n giggle and call me *'Gaijin! Gaijin!'* but not in any sorta mean way, but kinda like ther jokin' 'n real happy 'n I didn't mind atall. But I wuz ther thru the summer as well, 'n did poorly in the heat. T'aint the heat that gits ta ya, mind ya, but that humidity all pourin' down my back 'n face 'n my face turnin' all red. My face wuz all red all summer 'n on accounta my red face 'n my big nose, well those kids're startin' ta call me *'Tengu! Tengu!'* Tooka good look in the mirror when I got home 'n sher enuff, I'm the spittin' image of the *tengu* I saw the uther night on the *Mukashi-banashi* program fer kids 'n I laughed out loud."

"Ara ma ha! ha! Pittari janai no! That's what I will call you too. Even though you are not so red in the face, but it suits you perfectly, Mr. Tengu."

"Please, no need fer fermalities! Jist call me Tengu."

"Do you speak some Japanese? Are you, perhaps, a scholar?"

"Sher enuff. I reckon ya've a bit a sight if ya kin figger that out by jist lookin' at me 'n talkin'. Sher, I speak a bit Japanese, *sukōshi dake,* ya know. I wasn't in Japan fer strickly pleasure, tho my studies're a pleasure in thimselves, but that's anuther matter ultogether."

"Tell me of your studies. I wanted to be a scholar once, but I decided to be an old woman when I grew up. You can channel your life in several directions, but I wanted to focus on one thing only. And do it very well. I'm the best old woman you're going to find for many years to come!"

"Yer aint kiddin'! Yer so good at being an old woman, never even noticed it. Not many people kin do that, I reckon. I ain't so focussed as all that 'n bin dabblin' my fingers in a coupla pies."

"Well?"

"Well, whut?"

"Whut—What were you studying with so much pleasure in Japan?"

"Oh, I wuz doin' a comparitiv study on the origins 'n developminta Japanese *enka* 'n if ther any parallels with the developminta country 'n western in North America."

"Ehhhh. I never would have thought to make that connection. That's an interesting notion."

"Thank ya kindly. 'N whut did ya have in that ther sack, anyways?"

"Beer?"

"Sher, don't mind if I do. By the ways, whut wer ya wantin' me ta call ya?"

"Mmmmm. *Sō da ne.* Call me Purple."

"Purple, huh? Well it suits a funny little thing like ya, no disrespect intended ya kin have anuther smoke if ya want."

"Yes, thank you. They taste so *natsukashii,* after twenty dry years of prairie dust."

"I reckon anythin'd taste *natsukashii* after twenty years. Jist help yerself to my smokes, all ya want, I don't mind atall."

"You're a good person, Tengu. And it's nice to meet you after all this time. *Kanpai!*"

"Kanpai!" Tengu says, and clangs his beer can against mine. We drink and it warms our bellies. Tengu's face begins to turn a lovely shade of red.

"Yer welcome ta stay on as long as ya like. I don't reckon I've ever picked up an interestin' hitch-hiker as ya, not that yer ixackly hitchin' but I wouldn't mind ya stayin' on. Gits a mite borin' drivin' by yerself in the snow, don't know 'bout walkin'. Can ya drive a stick?"

"Sher."

"I think this is gonna be fun! Ya know?"

"Thank you, Tengu. I like you very much and I'm very much ready for fun. Do you want some dried squid?"

"Sher!"

The chew champ craw of dried salted squid and good company to share it with. I'm content. There was a time when a body couldn't dare hitch a ride with a stranger wearing a battered straw cowboy hat all bent and finger-creased. Maybe a hundred years ago. Maybe tomorrow. But today, today it is fine. Listen, listen, how the snow scrapes across the windshield, the surface of the truck. *Fubuki,* I guess. So dense, so thick we leave eddies behind and solitary trucks that pass before, why, the headlights scatter across facets of snow and reflect the brightness skyward. Imagine! I've been picked up by a Tengu who smokes Mild Seven cigarettes and is a cowboy music scholar! Yes, today is fine, indeed. So nice to feel light in soul, in mind and nothing to mar my pleasure. Having the space to choose my own companions. I can't think of a finer place to be than inside the warm and smoky cab of a pick-up truck. Horse sweet smell of sweat and hay. Drinking beer with a new-found friend. Funny how it takes twenty long years to take one step outside, then, you manage to take more steps than you ever have in your life. That all you have to do is move your body from one place to another and everything around you changes so much, you have to grow new eyes, new ears. To see and hear. You have to grow a new mouth. I'm not too old to change. I leave Murasaki behind, but she must shape her own location. And our stories entwine and loop around and this will never change. She lingers here, with me, even now.

(Naoe: Murasaki?

Murasaki: Yes, Obāchan?

Naoe: I just wanted to hear your thoughts.

Murasaki: Nice. Obāchan, are you fine?

Naoe: Yes, Murasaki. There is beer in my belly and good conversation lingers in my ears. I have met a friend and my toes are warm.

Murasaki: I'm glad, Obāchan.

Naoe: Thank you.)

"Yer quite the one fer mutterin' to yerself tho I sher shouldn't talk, when I bin drivin' on my own fer a whiles, I kin really chat up a storm with no one but myself, but yer talkin' ta someone else completely weren't ya?"

"Yes, I talk with my *mago*, my granddaughter. Though 'talk' might not be the way to describe what we do. We share with each other, even when our bodies are far apart."

"Ya some kinda psychic or telepath or I dunno, one a those or ya jist kinda talkin' metuphorickly?"

"Maybe a little of everything?"

"Sher. Sher. There'd be alot more stranger things in this world'n that 'n I kinda wish I could do that too, wouldn't mind chattin' with my ma now 'n then but if it goes both ways, I s'ppose she'd start peerin' into my head more'n I liked, that's jist the type of gal she is, more power to her, but I s'ppose I like ta keep my thoughts to myself 'til I bother ta spill 'em outta my mouth, ya know?"

"Yes, I do know. I know exactly what you mean."

"I think I'm gittin' a tad sleepy, not 'cause of present company, jist bin drivin' fer a good solid stretch 'n that beer right tuckered me out. Don't mind me yawnin' 'cause it ain't 'cause yer borin' me."

"Don't worry about me, Tengu. I'm fine. I think I'm finer than I've ever been in my life. Why don't I tell you a story to keep you awake. That is, if you like that sort of thing."

"I'd love it," he says, and his smile is beautiful.

Mukāshi, mukāshi, ōmukashi . . .

Deep, deep in the mountain forest, there lived a *yamanba* who lived by herself in a small house of her own making. Being a mountain woman, she was very very strong and had thick arms and legs like the root of the *daikon.* She lived quietly, tending her small garden where she planted burdock and *satoimo* during the day, and at night, she lingered by the fire in the *irori,* sipping from a jug of *sake* and reading from her books. She did not care for the company of humans, because they were small and bothersome. She just watched the birds in the trees and picked mushrooms in the forest. Her life with herself was complete and she felt little need ever to change it.

One day, the *yamanba* strayed farther from her mountain home than she usually cared to travel. Trees swayed as she passed, her feet shook the ground beneath her. But despite her giant size, she walked carefully. Careful not to tred on the things smaller than herself. The giant woman was looking for someone to talk to. Endless seasons had passed since she had left her mountain home, and the books she read were starting to crumble to dust. There was change in the air, she had smelled it for quite some time, but had chosen not to heed it.

As she came down the mountain, she saw that the trees were sickly. That there wasn't a hum of insect chatter, and the brooks were sluggish and choked. The stench in her nose brought bile to her throat, and she blinked back the salt in her eyes. Wherever she looked, there was only the silence of dead and dying things. The earth was too beaten to weep. The *yamanba* saw something churn at her feet, and she crouched low and peered closely. It was a maggot.

"Little Maggot, tell me what has happened to the land?"

"Elder Sister, you are late. Late to come down from your mountain."

"Where are the green things, the water and the breeze?"

"They are gone away, away. I don't know why. My brothers and sisters are eating their bones. When there is nothing more to eat, we will go away too."

"Tell me, Little Maggot, where are my sisters? Where have the other mountain women gone to so that I may join them?"

"We ate their bones yesterday. We ate them yesterday. And we will eat you tomorrow. That is the way of maggots."

"Yes, that is the way of maggots, but it is not for me to be eaten tomorrow. Little Friend, eat a little less today, so you do not eat me tomorrow."

"Why do you want to stay when your sisters have gone away? You will be lonely with no words to hear, no ears to speak your sounds to."

"I am a *yamanba* and I am strong. I will speak my words aloud and shape the earth again. If you choose to listen, I will tell you stories."

"What have you to say that we would care to hear? We

churn in the bones of the dead. What have we to do with living things?"

"Are you not one of the living as well?" the *yamanba* asked softly.

"Yes," the maggot said, after some thought. "I guess we are."

"If you eat of the dead, the conclusion of the cycle is your death. That is all that remains."

"The marrow we eat is dry and bitter, but we do not wish to die. Yet."

"Then come," the *yamanba* beckoned. She lay upon the silent ground and tilted back her head. Opened wide her great mouth, and the maggots churned in the soil around her. They squirmed and squiggled on to her body, covering her in their glowing whiteness. An undulating blanket. They trickled and streamed into her mouth, down, down her throat. And more and more and so many more, they moiled out of the dying earth. The maggots filed on and on, so many that she couldn't possibly hold them all, but still she let them enter. When the last one flipped over the edge of her lip, she heaved a great sigh and closed her mouth. Swallowed. She heard the whispering clamour of millions of tiny voices shouting from her belly.

"Hurry! Hurry! There is no room inside here. We are tender and the walls of your stomach scrape us so. We want to leave! Please, hurry, hurry," the maggots cried, wriggling in their discomfort. The *yamanba* rose to her feet, tottering a little with the added weight. Stood tall upon the earth. Her feet planted like stone, she swung her great breasts out of her *samui* and clenched two fists around them. She milked her breasts with great white spurts and a steady stream of maggots squirted from her nipples. When the maggots touched the earth, they squirmed, swelled, flipped about at her feet. Their bodies grew longer and taller and limbs began to form. Fingers, hands, calves and feet. Some were tall and slender while others stayed plump and soft. They grew and clamoured around her. In wonder, they called her mother. When the *yamanba* squeezed the last maggots from her breasts, there were millions of soft-skinned people around her.

"You are weak, but soon your skin will bake to lovely shades of brown and the sun will not bother you so. Some will never brown like your hardy companions, so you must take care each other. Remember you were maggots. If you do not take care, you will fall back into the habit of eating the dead."

The *yamanba* was weary, but she had to care for her maggot children. She turned to the stream that flowed with sluggish thickness, and hunkered down beside it. She knelt, and dipped her face to the sickly stench and pursed her giant lips. She sucked the water back and back, sucked with great strength. The dirty water filled her mouth but she swallowed on and on. She sucked the stream dry. When she was finished, she moved slowly, the water jostling inside her from side to side, and straddled the dry riverbed with both feet. She squatted, with a grunt and let loose. Jaaaaaaa. Jaaaaaaaaaaaaa. The water rushed from her body, jaaaaaaaaa in a steady stream between her muscular thighs. But the water was no longer sickly, it was crystal clear. The water flowed, sweet and pure between her legs. The maggot people were soothed by the sound of the sparkling liquid. Dipped their fingers in the stream.

"It's good! The water is sweet!" they cried and splashed about in the stream in joy. When droplets of water fell on the earth, flowers and trees and delicate mushrooms burst from the ground in great profusion. The growth of green and tender things spread outward in a circle. Soon, the earth was fresh again, and the water flowed like music. The *yamanba* smiled as the maggot children danced with their new bodies around her. It began to rain.

"That was a lovely story," he says, tugging the brim of his finger-smudged cowboy hat.

"Thank you."

"I don't suppose you'll tell me what happened to the maggot children and the *yamanba*, huh?"

"Ah, but that's another tale."

"I thought you'd say that," he sighs in exaggerated sadness.

"Ara?"

"What's the matter?" he asks, jerks his head up to glance quickly at my face. His foot instinctively lifts from the accelerator.

"What happened to your accent?" I am amazed. And confused.

"What accent?" he says, his brow puckered up.

"Your cowboy western drawl accent."

"I never had an accent. At least not one I noticed," he grins.

"Ehhhhhhh."

"What's wrong?" Tengu asks, smiling crinkles into the corners of his eyes.

"I feel so strangely. Here I was, listening to you with an accent in my ears, only there might not have been one on your lips. And it makes me wonder what else we filter through our ears. And how can anyone be sure if what they hear is what is said?" If I think about it too long, my head will burst, I'm certain!

"You shouldn't be so fussy," Tengu says, tugging the rim of his hat. "Besides, it doesn't matter now, because it's in your head already. That's as real as it's going to get."

"Yes, you could be right. Do you have any more Mild Sevens?"

"I got a whole carton in that bag, there at your feet," Tengu nods.

"Well, that shows that I'm not making everything up. Some of it must be true."

Murasaki

He cooked for me with casual grace and I just sat at the table with an icy bottle of cheap *sake*, my clumsy feet on the chair beside me. I was content. It wasn't that I didn't like to cook, only that it was such a pleasure to watch someone who did it so gracefully. I am from the school of cooks who go red in the face and leave debris all around me. I do, of course, like to eat. And he fed me well. He pared radishes with a deft hand, twirled the blade of his slice sharp knife and a carrot turned into a rose. I quietly applauded his magic act. With delicate ease, he slivered pickled ginger into paper-thin slices and gently teased the rich-fleshed tuna to part from knobby bone. Slid knife through squid so thin so fine, the meat shone pearl opaque. I ate. Fresh seaweed so green it squeaked between my molars, ruby slices of tuna and gleam of fresh squid so sweet so chewy and hot! green mustard tingle tingled up my nose and to my head, quick, quick, sipped some icy *sake*, my face burned with delight. Obāchan, I tasted for you.

"You're not holding your chopsticks quite properly," he said.

"I know. I don't hold my pen properly either. But I can still write. And I can still eat." I dipped some squid into my tiny dish of *shōyu* and *wasabi,* turned it over once to cover it completely. Lifted the piece up to my mouth. My *hashi* wobbled slightly and I dribbled sauce down my chin, but the squid was in my mouth and it was oh so sweet. I was wiping the sauce off my chin with my fingers when he grabbed my hand. Licked them. He licked my fingers and slid tongue palm, nipped the heel with sharp prickle suck oh! oh! swirled circles with tongue, my palm, his teeth. Skin licked smooth and scrape, scraped edge of teeth, edge of skin, oh! Buttons. The exquisite infinite pleasure of buttons, slow twist of button out of button hole and swirled fingers dipped and stroked and whispered on heated skin on moist moist. The flat of palms slid. Slid down the slick heat of my breasts, my belly. I ran my fingers down the front of his shirt, buttons popping open, tugged his pants, no time to linger, oh hurry, hurry, kicked off my jeans, laughing, tumbling to the floor. He rolled with me on the floor, rolling, him on top then me then him. Rolling until there is no top or bottom, only a dizzy spiral of pleasure. The table, the chairs, the *sushi,* all spinning in the air above us.

It was hard growing up in a small prairie town, the only Japanese-Canadians for miles around. Where everybody thought Japan was the place they saw when they watched "Shōgun" on TV. Obāchan laughed when she saw it. I thought it was a good story.

We were parked at S-coulee, drinking lemon gin. I had opened his clumsily wrapped present and now his hands were inside my blouse and mine around his neck. He smelled like Dial soap.

"Do you like the T-shirt?" Hank asked.

"Yes, thank you. I'm sorry, I didn't get you a present for our three week anniversary."

"You could give me something now."

"Oh Hank. I already told you, I don't want to go all the way yet."

"We don't have to. Aren't there special things you can do without going all the way?" he asked, looking at me with half-closed eyes.

"What do you mean, special things?"

"You know," he said, squirming in his trousers. "Like Oriental sex."

"What's Oriental sex?" This was a first.

"I don't know. *You* should know. You're Oriental aren'tchya?" He was getting grouchy with my obtuseness, my unlearned innate sexuality.

"Not really," I said. "I think I'm Canadian."

"Ahhh, you don't have to be embarrassed. I won't tell anybody if we do stuff."

"What stuff?" I was going to lose it. And Hank was really nice, at heart, too.

"You know. The Oriental kinky stuff. Like on 'Shōgun'."

"Oh yeah," I said, tucking my blouse back into my jeans.

"Hey, where are you going?"

I threw the T-shirt anniversary present in his face. I didn't even know why I was so mad.

"Hyuck, hyuck," I said.

"Are you laughing in your sleep or are you awake?" he asked.

"I'm awake," I said, stroking his smooth chest with lazy fingers.

"What's so funny?"

"Oh, I was just remembering my first real boyfriend."

"When you were at university?" Curious with a lover's desire to hear of intimacy before him.

"No!" I laughed. "Junior high school!"

"*Ehhhhhh.* Boy, you really start young around here."

"I guess. I can't speak for all the small towns, but most places that are small, there isn't much to do except drink and have sex. Or at least make out."

"Did you have sex with your first real boyfriend?" he asked, lying on his side with his chin in the curve of his palm. Facing me.

"Nah. I might have if he hadn't pissed me off, but he did. Besides, he had terrible taste in T-shirts. How old were you when you had a real girlfriend?"

"As old as I am now," he smiled.

"Are you trying to be cute?"

"I would never be cute for you."

"Do you want to have Oriental sex?" I asked, posing in what I thought could be seen as an Oriental gesture.

"What's Oriental sex?"

"I don't know," I answered, "but I thought I would make it up as I go along."

"Let's make it up together."

I was, of course, snubbed by everyone for two weeks. Even Julie, even Patricia, couldn't forgive me, he had bought me a present after all.

"You're too touchy," Julie hissed. She wasn't even supposed to be talking to me but she was too furious to keep up the silent treatment.

"What's your problem, anyways? Hank's all broken up about you and he didn't even do anything! You blew it and no one's going to go out with you now."

That, at least, turned out to be true. I never went out with another Nanton boy ever again. I messed around with a couple of out of town boys from High River and Vulcan. But not for keeps. Meanwhile, my Oriental hormones were running rampant, so to speak. Hard to grow up in agricultural hell, in cowboy purgatory.

"What's happened to Hank? He never calls anymore and I haven't seen him for at least two weeks, I'm sure," Mom said.

"News flash! Muriel Tonkatsu and Hank Hardy broke up three weeks ago. Tap tap taptaptaptap."

"Oh Muriel! He was such a nice boy too, even though his family goes to the Church of Christ. What happened?"

"Nothing you'd care to hear about."

"That's no way to talk! Of course I care about what's going on in your life! Any mother would. You know you can talk to me about anything."

"Mom, he wanted to have Oriental sex with me."

"Oh, well, the Bible says we should wait, ummmm. . ." she trailed away.

Obāchan and I, our eyes collided, and we began to laugh. Mom's pots and pans a clattering chorus behind us.

Our family wasn't the only "Oriental" family in town. There was Joe and his wife, Jane, and the many other Vietnamese workers at the farm whom I hardly knew at all. Whom I never knew. And there were Chinese-Canadians who'd been around, I was certain, forever. Jim Wu's family who ran Ginger Jim's on Main Street and Mrs. Ching with no Mr. Ching. She had three daughters who helped run the grocery store until they left, one by one, to run a gas station in Winnipeg, manage a condominium in Edmonton, and enter law school out east. I don't know the names of the Ching girls, they graduated when I was just getting into junior high. I only heard stories of what they did when they left town. I knew they went to the same school as I because their class graduation pictures hung on the walls in the hallway. Wearing lilac long dresses with puffed sleeves and thick, framed glasses. Looking like decades ago. I couldn't connect the photos I saw with the stories I had heard. The Ching girls were long gone and I envied them their escape from rural hell.

Jim Wu had four kids, and one of his sons was a year older than me. His name was Shane. Shane Wu. And god, I felt sorry for him, having to live with his name in a cowboy town. With his Asian face. When he was short and tubby with big hands and feet so he looked uncomfortable all the time. Having a name like Shane, playing hockey, but only as a second string goalie. And I never talked with him in my entire life. He never talked with me. Instinct born of fear, I knew that being seen with him would lessen my chances of being in the popular crowd. That Oriental people in single doses were well enough, but any hint of a group and it was all over. I thought I was proud of being Japanese-Canadian, but I was actually a coward. I don't know what Shane's reasons were for never talking with me. I never asked.

But we held hands, once, when I was in grade six and he was in grade seven. June, when the clouds swell thick and black from the west and squeeze through the foothills. Around nine at night, and I was riding my bike in town, on my way home from eating supper at Julie's house. Shane was on the sidewalk, on his way to the restaurant to help his father clean up and close down. The sky crackled dark and sudden and the lightning was right on top of us. The wind was mad, raising dust devils, little pellets of stone. There was a sizzle/crack! and all the streetlights went out. I fell off my bike. I must have yelped or something and Shane stumbled toward me, his foot bumping into my bike. It was so absolutely dark, I couldn't see his face, I only saw his hand out for me to grab. The lightning scorching the air around us. I reached and Shane pulled me up. I bent down to get my bike, held it up with my right hand, and clutched Shane's hand with my left. It was darker than an eclipse, or something, I don't know why, but it was dark enough for me to hold Shane's hand. He walked me home, in the wind and rain, a mile and a half south west of town. My hand in his, his hand in mine, the wind howling like demons. He never said a single thing and I didn't say anything either, only pushed my bike awkwardly with my right hand. When he saw me to my door, he turned around without saying good-bye and walked a mile and a half back into town.

I don't know what happened to Shane. He quit school when he finished grade eleven, I never found out why. His picture doesn't hang in the hallway of the school. His story isn't mine to speak.

(Murasaki: Obāchan?

Naoe: *Hai?*

Murasaki: Obāchan, I don't know what to say anymore. I don't know what to ask. Does it even matter?

Naoe: I can't give you any answers, child. I'm just beginning to find answers of my own. But listen. Why don't I talk sometimes and you just move your lips and it will look like you're the one who's talking.

Murasaki: That's a great idea, Obāchan. Thanks.

Naoe: Not at all. You can do the same for me, sometimes.

Murasaki: Sure, Obāchan. I could surely do that.)

When Obāchan left our home forever, Mom had a nervous breakdown. Well, nothing diagnosed or formally said, she just refused to leave her room. She stayed in bed for three months and never opened the curtains. Never turned on the lights. I stayed home from school to take care of her, nothing I was too pleased to do, after all, I was in high school and on the basketball team and not too hot at math, either. I couldn't afford to miss school if I wanted to keep my grades. But for once in his life, Dad insisted.

"You will stay home to care for your mother." Dad, who never ordered a thing in his life! He couldn't even order food at a restaurant, let alone make a command on anyone's life. I was so shocked, I didn't even make a fuss. It was arranged I would make up any lost work during the summer holidays. So I stayed home, watched over Mom and tried to make her eat. She just lay like a log in the middle of her bed. At least she got up to pee. At least she didn't shit her pants. But something changed in me, during the time I spent in the dark with a silent mother. Mother in name but a total stranger. A place I had never tried to move beyond. I wasn't free from guilt.

She did get up to pee, but she didn't take a bath. I had to wipe her with a towel to keep her clean. At first, she wore a nightie, like she always did, but I had a hell of a time, propping her body up to get it over her head whenever I wanted to bathe her or change her clothes. And she didn't try to help. She just lay limply, no words passed her lips. Then I got a brain wave. I ran to Obāchan's room, the same as when she left it, rummaged through her drawers and came up with her *nemaki* Japanese night clothes. They were made like robes, and the front was only wrapped around the body to be tied at the sides so that the whole thing could be taken off without pulling anything over the head. I took one into to Mom's room and held it up.

"Look Mom, this is just perfect! Now we won't have to jostle you around so much. It'll be easier to change your clothes and give you a bath, okay?" I didn't expect her to say anything, she hadn't said anything for ten days, the day since Obāchan left.

"O. . . K."

I was shocked. But I tried not to look surprised.

"Dad said he'd be home early tonight, they're casing, and picking should just be a half day. There's supposed to be a chinook tomorrow. It's about time, it was so cold this morning Dad had to kick the front door open because it was all caked with ice at the bottom. Actually, it's kinda nice staying home in the winter like this, I mean, it's too cold to even think." I chatted away, hoping it would make Mom want to talk to me, but she didn't say anything else.

"Dad, Mom talked today!" He had come in from the farm, and I was in the kitchen, making macaroni and cheese.

"Really?! What did she say?"

"She said, 'O. . . K'."

"That's it?" Disappointed.

"At least it's something! At least you don't have to sit around here all day in a dark and stinkin' house with no one to talk to except yourself and a woman who's turned into a house plant! She should get professional help, but no, make the daughter lose her mind as well. After ten days, I think that 'O. . . K' is a bloody breakthrough!"

I was waiting for Dad to yell or shake me or something. After ten long days of winter silence, I wanted something to explode. But he didn't say anything. He opened his arms wide and I fell into them for the first time.

"Thank you, Muriel," he said, the words vibrating in his chest, and my throat swelled with salty tears.

After that, I thought Mom might start talking a little. Make a slow progress. But she fell back into silence and nothing I said could make her talk again. I was crushed. I had had visions of me going back to school and parties on weekends and basketball tournaments, but the future looked dim and I became depressed. Not the ideal emotional state for someone who is trying to nurse someone else out of a depression. The house became a hollow thing, the only noise was the sound of dust snaking across the wooden floors. After all those years of Obāchan's voice. Her language of memory, pain, desire. The silence in our home was so complete our ears rang with the sudden loss of sound. I turned my thoughts inward, and inward yet again.

(Murasaki: Obāchan! Obāchan! OBĀCHAN!

Naoe: *Ara! Murasaki-chan?*

Murasaki: Obāchan?

Naoe: *Hai! Obāchan da yo. Dōshita no, sonnani ōkina koe o dashite?*

Murasaki: Oh, Obāchan. Am I losing my mind? I can understand what you're saying, and how can we be talking anyway?! I must be insane.

Naoe: *Ara,* Murasaki, that doesn't sound like the granddaughter I know and love. There are stranger things in life than two people who are close being able to understand one another.

Murasaki: Yeah, but over distance and time? Not to mention life. You're dead after all, aren't you?

Naoe: Of course not! As if I would be ready for death.

Murasaki: But what about the snow? The high windchill factor and everything? There were search parties out for a week and no one found a trace.

Naoe: If an old woman chooses to leave, it's an easy enough thing to cover one's tracks. Dead! *Mattaku!*

Murasaki: Sorry. But you have to admit, you kinda shocked everyone. Especially Mom. She's kinda lost it.

Naoe: *Ara.* Is she all right?

Murasaki: No. Not really. I think she's had a bit of a nervous breakdown.

Naoe: *Ara-raaa.* I'm so sorry. It must be hard for you. But harder yet on Keiko. She is so strong of mind, stronger than even me, that she must be awfully hurt to hide inside herself. You must help her, Murasaki.

Murasaki: I've been trying. Not very gracefully.

Naoe: You must try harder. What have you been feeding her?

Murasaki: Well, macaroni and cheese. Hot dogs. Stuff like that.

Naoe: *Mattaku!* Of course she won't be getting better on food such as that! Have a little sense!

Murasaki: Gee, sorry Obāchan! It's not as if I ever learned to cook or anything.

Naoe: Don't be sarcastic! Just listen.

Murasaki: Okay.)

"You switch around in time a lot," you say, a bowl of coffee resting in your palms. "I get all mixed up. I don't know in what order things really happened." You lift the coffee to your lips and slurp at hot liquid. Nibble a dry Italian biscuit and look expectantly up at me.

I tip my chai to my lips, and lick sweet aromatic milk that lingers. I want to just ignore you. You with your dry biscuits and expectations. But it would be rude and you have listened with care and intelligence. You have participated in the story.

"There isn't a time line. It's not a linear equation. You start in the middle and unfold outward from there. It's not a flat surface that you walk back and forth on. It's like being inside a ball that isn't exactly a ball, but is really made up of thousands and thousands of small panels. And on each panel, there is a mirror, but each mirror reflects something different. And from where you crouch, if you turn your head up or around or down or sideways, you can see something new, something old, or something you've forgotten."

"Wow," you say. "Wow, that sounds like some mind bend. Some people might call it madness."

"Yeah, I guess. But some might call it magic."

"Abracadabra," you say. "Shazam! Presto! Open Sesame! Chi chin pui pui! I love peanut butter sandwiches!" you yell, waving your arms in a vaguely mysterious fashion. Everyone in the coffee shop is staring at you and I laugh and laugh until I am crying.

"Dad," I said, cutting up some fruit and mixing it with yogurt, "you have to watch Mom for a while today. I need the car to do some shopping in Calgary."

"Farm's busy. Icy highway. Maybe another day?"

"Dad, I insist."

"Okay, Muriel."

The highway spun away from the tires of the car. Alone and enjoying every second of it. The snaking paths of snow twining on the surface of the road. The thrill of driving fast in dangerous conditions. I had the radio blasting and singing so loudly I couldn't hear the hum of the car or the wind roaring against it.

I didn't even notice the cop car had his flashing lights on, didn't notice him until he pulled up beside me and turned on his siren and I was so surprised I swerved a little into his lane and he had to veer away into oncoming traffic to avoid a collision.

"Shit!" I hissed. "Oh shit oh shit oshit!" as I slowed down, turned off my radio, and pulled over to the side.

The officer got out of his patrol car, shiny boots first, and his face was red with what I could only hope was his natural skin colour.

"You're in a lot of trouble. I clocked you at 148 and you were driving dangerously and I can also nail you for resisting an officer. You'll lose your licence, if you're old enough to even have one, and the fine is liable to pop your daddy's eyes outta his head. Let's see your licence. And your registration and insurance."

I didn't say anything at all, just handed him the papers. He slowly flipped through them, went back to his car and called up headquarters, or wherever on his radio, looking up now and then, to stare at the back of my head. He returned ominously slowly.

"So, you're Muriel Tonkatsu, huh. You lost your grandmother a while ago, the word says. Sorry to hear that. I guess I can go easy on you this time. You're probably under a lot of stress and all. But I'm still giving you a speeding ticket. Can't have you speeding in weather conditions like this. Just take care not to turn on the radio so loud."

And he smiled, actually smiled when he gave me the ticket. Not a mean smile, not a condescending one, just a nice and friendly smile. It made me feel so sorry, for I don't know what, that tears pooled in my eyes, and I had to blink and blink so that they wouldn't spill over.

I drove more slowly, after that, and turned down the volume on the radio. Stayed in the right-hand lane, flicked on my lights. Checked the map tacked on the visor and exited at Marquis de Lorne Trail, or whatever. Follow the airport signs until you hit Seventeenth Avenue SE, then turn right then take the next left at the first intersection, Dad had told me. I don't know how he knew where the place was. After all, it wasn't like he ever went shopping there, was it? I mean we never had a single Japanese food item in our house, aside from Obāchan's packages from Japan. Why would Dad know the Oriental Food Store when he's never bought anything Oriental in his whole immigrant life? Has he? And Obāchan. How did Obāchan know about it? "Go to the Oriental Food Store in south east Calgary," she says. "Ask your father for directions." It wasn't like she ever left the house, or anything. Was it? But no time to think of things I couldn't figure out anyway. The traffic on Deerfoot Trail careened around me with a blast of horn, a splash of slush, and no windshield wiper fluid. I just hummed myself into safety and periodically slammed on my brakes when people drove too close behind me.

Tinkle tinkle of door, the sound was soothing after my palm-sweat stress of driving on a busy highway. I stood in the doorway and breathed in deep the scent of spices foreign to my senses. I was bemused.

"Hello, you must be Sam Tonkatsu's daughter, I can see the family resemblance, nice to meet you." She stood firm and solid behind the cash register, wearing a white apron that covered her from neck to mid-thigh. Her head perched on top like a snow woman. She smiled hugely, and her teeth were comfortingly crooked.

"Hi," I said, and kind of waved, for the lack of anything better to do. I was shocked. Dad came here? To this store?

"How's your Dad doing? I haven't seen him come around for a couple of weeks now. He must be getting low on his salted seaweed paste."

"Dad eats salted seaweed paste?" my mouth dropped open.

"Funny guy, your Dad. Never says much and all he ever buys is salted seaweed paste. Try some pickled radish, I tell him. Try some of our specialty *rāmen,* I say. But no, all he ever buys is the seaweed."

"Did my Mom come here too?" I asked, starting to doubt the things I saw with my eyes, heard with my ears, as truth. "Did she ever buy anything too?"

"Not that I know of. Didn't even know Sam had a daughter until I saw you walk in the door. But you couldn't be anyone else. You look like he would have looked when he was younger, only with a wig."

"Gee, thanks a lot. That's very descriptive."

"Wa! ha! ha! haaa!" she laughed enormously. "That

wasn't meant as an insult, dear! He's quite a striking man, and you're an interesting looking girl."

"Oh good, this gets better and better."

"Wa! ha! ha! haaa! Is there anything I can help you with?"

"Yeah, actually. I have a list here, somewhere." I patted my back pocket and pulled out a folded piece of foolscap.

miso
katsuobushi
wakame
konbu
mirin
nori
natto
yamaimo
sanma
ika
kome

takuwan
shōga
tōfu
hakusai
daikon
shōyu
furikake
satoimo
aji no hiraki
tonkatsu sauce
rāmen

"That's some list," she said, peering over my shoulder and breathing quite heavily into my hair. "Run out of the staples, huh?"

"I wouldn't know. My Obāchan gave me the list, and I know what the words mean, but I have no idea what they are."

"Isn't that some sort of aphasia? Were you in an accident or something? Maybe it's personal, huh. Tell me if I'm being too pushy."

"Pardon?" There were too many things swirling in my head.

"Never mind, I'll help you out."

"By the way," something occurred to me. "The *tonkatsu* in *tonkatsu* sauce?"

"Yes?"

"Is that the same *tonkatsu* like my name?"

"You mean you don't know?" She was amazed.

"No, I guess I don't." I felt my face glow warmer, but I had to know.

"Maybe you should ask your Dad," she said, shooting price stickers on the bottom of a few cans, glancing up at my face between every tha-chunk. "I'm not sure of the origins and such. It could have a totally different character spelling. Or it could be a nickname that turned into a real name."

"I don't know if he remembers. Please tell me. I want to know now." I was so close to a different understanding, I could almost taste it.

"Well, the only *tonkatsu* I'm familiar with is a food."

"Oh boy," I muttered, I don't know if I can stand another shock.

"It's a type of breaded deep-fried pork cutlet."

"Ohmygod."

"I think it's very unique and interesting. Maybe your father's family was in the food or restaurant business. Who knows, maybe his family invented them!" she expanded, warming to the subject.

"I can't stand it."

"There's nothing nicer than a *tonkatsu* dinner on a cold winter evening. It fills you up and everyone eats them licketysplit. Everyone loves *tonkatsu.* Don't tell me you've never had one."

"I've never had one."

"Well!" she said, outraged, "well, it just won't do!" She bustled to the meager book and magazine rack and flipped through a stack. Chose a thin, colour photo recipe book of Japanese food and smacked it against her thigh. Dust flew and made me sneeze twice.

"Take this. On the house. You learn how to make *tonkatsu* and you eat them up. Make your Obāchan proud of you."

"Thanks!" I flipped through the pages, the photographs making my mouth water for things I'd never tasted.

"Put that down for now," she said. "I'll show you what you've got on that shopping list of yours."

I tagged after her, pushing a shopping cart. Pausing in front of the small produce section, and pointing to certain vegetables, she said the words aloud.

"Daikon." *Big white radish thing as long as my forearm.*

"Hakusai." *Leafy frilly cabbage thing I've seen in Safeway.*

"Shōga." *Fresh root of ginger, translation not literal.*

"Satoimo." *Little fur covered balls, root vegetable, no tuber.*

"Don't worry, once you eat what they are, you won't forget them," she swept through the aisles, dropping items into the shopping cart.

"Mirin, nori, miso. . . . The recipe book should help. Is your mom white?"

"No, she just doesn't make Japanese food."

"Oh, that's too bad. Eating's a part of being after all. How many pound of rice do you want?"

"Oh, just a couple for now, I guess."

"They only come in twenty-five or fifty pound bags."

"Oh," I said blushing, embarrassed of my ignorance. "The twenty-five pound bag, then. What was it you said my Dad bought all the time?"

"Salted seaweed paste. Excellent on hot rice."

"I'll have some of that too."

"Okay. I think that about covers your list." She started ringing it through the till. I was overwhelmed. The strange but familiar food. Dad and his seaweed. Our name.

"That'll be $187.49."

"Good god!"

"It gets pricey. Most of it's imported you know. Can't be helped. Did you bring enough money?"

"I was going to treat myself to a movie and maybe a new pair of jeans, but I guess that's out."

"You can put some stuff back if you want," she raised her heavy eyebrows. "I don't mind ringing it through the till again, we're not so busy."

"Nah, it's all right. I should go home before it gets dark, anyway."

"Here's your change. Let me help you out to your car." She swung the sack of rice over one shoulder and clutched a box beneath her other arm. The door tinkle tinkled. I popped open the trunk and set my box inside. As the woman put down the rice, I asked,

"What's your name anyway?"

"Sushi."

Nothing could surprise me now. I stuck out my hand.

"Thanks for all your help, Sushi."

She shook my hand briskly and rattled my head in the process.

"Tell me how the *tonkatsu* works out."

Naoe

Funny how I hated the wind so much when I was sitting still. I guess it is an easy thing to read what you will when you can see from only one side of your face. But a body can never be objective. There's always too much at stake. Easy now, to admire the wind, sitting inside a warm cab of a truck, beer in the belly, and a cigarette between my lips! I can almost hear the snow hissing across the icy highway. Snaking, swirling, it almost makes a body dizzy. Mesmerize.

"Tengu!"

"Huh—what?"

"You almost went into the ditch!"

"Oh, sorry." Rubs his knuckles across his eyes. "I guess I shouldn't have had that beer. I hope I didn't scare you."

"I think I should drive."

"You sure you know how to drive a stick?" He glances at me, one eyebrow higher than the other.

"Of course. Don't worry," I say, patting his shoulder. "Just leave the driving to me and you can get some sleep."

"If you're sure. I'm really beat." Tengu brakes slowly, slowly, shifting down with his hazards flashing for good measure. Not that anyone could see them in this whirlwind of snow. Without having crushed us already.

"Where are we going for now?" I ask. Not tied to destination. Only a grand departure.

"I don't know," he says, rubbing his chin. We are stopped and the wind is so strong, it rocks the truck from side to side. "Just go forwards, for now." He opens his door to get out and the blast of ice is so fast so cold, my nostrils crackle and the inside of the windshield freezes with a clang. I slide over to sit behind the wheel and pull the seat up as far as it will go. Tengu slams into where I had been sitting. Rubs his hands.

"Forwards it is," I say, and shift into first. "That's easy enough."

"Yeah, good night." And he is snoring so quickly, at first I think he is joking.

So thick with snow with ice, I can't hear the clamour of stars. Their voices are dimmed and scattered. Only this thickness of cold, the heap of clouds on top. So dark and muffled, I can't even see the lights of farm houses. There must be some out there. But straight ahead, I see an orange glow reflecting off the clouds. A hovering light above a city. Why, it must be Calgary! This must be the Calgary that everyone goes to. I suppose I must have been there once, getting off the airplane, but not long enough to remember. Calgary bathed in dull orange pallor, it's not a healthy complexion. Or, perhaps, a thousand thousand fishing boats floating on a snowy sea. Now that is a sweeter image.

I wonder if Tengu would mind if we stopped in Calgary. He said to go forward, but didn't say anything about having a little rest. Maybe I could eat some *tonkatsu.* No, I suppose it is too late for a good restaurant to be open. Except for a Smitty's or something, I don't know. And there's nothing there that I haven't been eating for the last twenty years! No offense to you, Keiko, but my tongue quivers for food of substance. The substance of memory. What is this MacLeod Trail? Lights after lights and still busy in the earliest hours of the morning. Such an obscenely sprawling road and it goes on for who knows how long? This MacLeod that the road was named after must have been a hefty garrulous man for the road to turn out so. *Mattaku!* Wait! I scent, a wonderful scent. Where is it coming from? I know! It must be Chinatown. For the people who dare to be hungry in the middle of the night. The starving hours before dawn. There must be one door that is open, for this scent to linger. Of course I know the food is not the same, but there is a compatibility of flavour, a simple nose tongue connection. Now if I can only make my way there. Well, I don't need a map. I'll just roll down my window and let the flavours of Chinatown beckon me. This roof of orange clouds above the city, at least it's good for something. At least it keeps the smells from seeping upward into space. Ahhhh, there. Yes, I can almost taste. Drive on, old woman, it is up ahead, drive on and this MacLeod Trail will end, I'm certain! Tengu sleeps like a baby, and such satisfied snoring! He must be tired, but I am not. No need for the elderly to sleep, they've spent so many years practicing at it, they can slumber wide awake at will. Or be wide awake when sleeping. It becomes one and the same and whispered stories are seldom ever missed. No, there is nothing in my will that would interest anybody, if I ever had written one anyway! *Ara!* What is that ahead? So many police cars and lights all red and swirling. It must be an accident. *Ara-maaa,* I hope no one has been injured. But why must we all stop?

Tap tap tap.

What! Tapping against the window with his flashlight so rude!

"Roll down your window, ma'am!" he yells against the icy pane of glass.

Mattaku! What is it now I wonder. When my belly is squeezing with hunger. I roll the window down a few centimetres to humour the shouting boy.

"Checkstop, ma'am. Have you been drinking this evening?"

"Have you no manners? Shining your flashlight in

people's faces and we can't even see yours let alone your badge and calling people ma'am and not even knowing if it's agreeable with them!"

". . . ."

"Have you nothing to say? I saw a flashlight somewhere, ah here it is and there you go, how do you like that? Not so pleasant to have light glaring in your face, now is it?"

"Sorry, miss, but I'll have to ask you to get out of your truck."

"Why, when I haven't done a thing and you so rude and smacking your flashlight against the window! Shining it in a body's eyes so there's nothing to see but spots!"

"I must insist. I wouldn't want to force you out."

"*Mattaku!* I would like to see you try. Never mind! Never mind! Don't get so red in the face. You'll burst something in your head well before your time. See, I'm out. Now what do you want before I catch a cold in this blizzard!"

"Walk on this line," he says, standing so close to me, I must look up to see his face.

"What?! Don't be ridiculous."

"Just do it, or we'll have to take you downtown for resisting an officer." He is smacking his flashlight against the side of his leg. We are not amused.

"You haven't even begun to see resistance, why—"

"Purple!"

"*Ara,* Tengu? Hard to sleep in all this fuss and lights. Sorry we had to wake you up when you were so tired. I'm having some trouble communicating with this young man, you just go back to sleep and I'll be back before you can say *chi chin pui pui!*"

"Purple, I think you should just walk along the white

line so we can get going again," Tengu is worried and he is raising and lowering his eyebrows quite madly.

"I will not! This person has been nothing but rude, no need to listen to a body just because he wears a silly uniform."

"Murasaki, kono hito no yū koto kikanai to taihen na koto ni naru yo. Ne? Tanomu kara," Tengu hisses, smiling all the while.

"Well, if you say so. But I still think he needs a good spanking."

"What did you say just now, to the woman?" the young officer asks, his mustache covering his childish lips.

"I told her the importance of obeying the law in a country not of her birth, officer."

"Yes, of course. These people should always remember that if they don't want any trouble. Go on, walk that line."

Chikishō! As if I'll walk a line for an unthinking man like you. I sweep my toe along the line and snap my elbows into my sides, my legs straight and toes pointed, my head a fulcrum, a point on a radius. Fling, leap my body into a side aerial. Graceful and weightless, I spin faster and faster, until my body's a blur and there is no ground, no sky. Only the white face of the officer spinning round and round like the moon. My legs a V but spinning so fast, I'm just a whirling circle. My elbows still tucked close into my sides, I swirl with speed, with grace. A huge gust of wind blows outward, upward, and all of the officers' hats fly up into the night sky. Old newspapers, discarded toques, mittens are gliding in the air. I land lightly, then step one foot out, toes gracefully pointed. Take a little bow. The officers' hats fall gently from the sky to land on their heads again and my young policeman has fainted, his eyes swirling. There is a light applause from the other officers, bedazzled with my show. "World class gymnast," they murmur and tip their hats to me. Like cowboys. Like Englishmen. Something Western, I'm certain. I just hop into the truck, snap Tengu's open mouth shut, and rev up the engine. Throw Western kisses as I drive away.

"You play a dangerous game, Purple. I was scared for you back there."

"Tengu, I have been sitting safe for so long— if I don't move against that grain, I will certainly be stuck there forever. Besides, I didn't like that young man. He had the look of a racist."

"How can you say something like that!" He is shocked.

"I don't know, I just got that feeling. It's a feeling that rarely lies. He had the kind of look that doesn't have any room for understanding or compassion or sympathy. Or love. That almost hidden tiny little sneer in the corner of the lip. Like he thinks he knows everything there is to know about you and doesn't like, will never like, what he sees. I guess that's what I mean about looking like a racist. I am not saying I've never been guilty myself. I'm not immune. It's harder to notice it on your own face. You have work extra hard to if you ever want to catch yourself."

"I guess, I know what you mean, maybe. But still, you ought to be careful you don't generalize. Be careful with the cops from now on, okay? And no more magic tricks! People will remember you. Unless you want to be remembered. But the way you were walking alone on the highway back there, it looked to me you were walking away from remembering," Tengu is looking stern, and so very endearing.

"As if it is ever possible. I found out a long time ago you

can never discard the past. It stays with you always. Let people remember me. There are worse things to remember than an old woman who can still play a few tricks."

"How did you do those flying cartwheel things anyway?"

"I'll never tell! Come, we're going to Chinatown for a feast. I'm paying."

"What's the celebration?" he smiles.

"I'll think of something."

"This is fantastic!" Tengu says, his mouth full of lobster meat, ginger pungent cream dripping from his lips. "I've never had lobster this good before." He licks his fingers from his pinkie to his thumb. It's good to see a body enjoy his food so much. I coax the meat from the pincers out with my chopsticks. What does "chopsticks" mean anyway? Who made it up? The world is cluttered and heaping with things untold and forgotten. But eat now, now is a time to eat. There is a time for words, but there is a time for food also. What can be more basic than that?

Ruby Restaurant. Well, more of a cafe, but the food is remarkable. There can be no complaints if you are hungry in the middle of the night and the door is open. Ahh, sip some tea. Eat. Crispy green *gai lan* and slightly bitter on my tongue. Shrimp and squid and scallop too, all salty crackle hot. And crispy mein, deep fried and such a sauce. My face all flush with taste, it fills the ache my belly has been missing after twenty long years of boiled beef and macaroni. Certainly, there were times when I had squid and *osenbei* too. And once I even made *sekihan* for Murasaki. But everything always from a cardboard box. Not spread before me on a table with so many choices, I don't know where to begin and steaming hot from the stove. Such food. It nourishes more than my body. I am replete.

"Can I offer you a beer?" Tengu asks, licking grains of salt from his lips.

"No," I say, heaping more lobster on to my plate. "I've had four tonight and I don't want to be so very drunk that I can't remember. But you go ahead if you like. I don't mind driving if you want to drive onward, or we can always find a hotel if we want to get some rest."

"You know, that might not be a bad idea. I kinda feel like having a couple beer and I've been sleeping in the cab of my truck for too long. Wouldn't mind taking a shower."

"Hotel it is, then! Why I haven't stayed in a hotel since I don't know when! So much fun in one night, I don't know if I can stand it. Do you have any money?" I ask.

"Yeah, I got some, but not very much. I have to ration it for gasoline, though. I don't want to be mooching from you, but do you have any?"

"Well, I have some cash, but I want to save it in case of an emergency. I really didn't want to use it until I was out of this province, but I think my credit card will be all right."

"Any particular reason you didn't want to use it in Alberta?" Tengu asks, reaching up to tug the brim of his cowboy hat, but he has politely taken it off when we sat down at the table, so there is nothing to tug.

"No need for you to worry about."

"If you're sure you won't get into any trouble," he says, his sun crinkle eyes concerned.

"Have another beer, Tengu."

"Don't mind if I do."

I eat, I drink. What more could a body ask for when there is shrimp, squid, scallops, and lobster heaped on plates before you? If I measured my happiness at this given moment, no one could be richer than me. Simple pleasure of crack crack lobster shell between my molars, pry sweet meat with my *hashi* and suck out the juice still inside, licking the garlic ginger cream sauce, pungent with green onions, and chew chew of lobster flesh, fresh and sweet as the sea. Sip, slurp from my cup of tea and choose a shrimp, a scallop. Pick up my rice bowl and tip some rice into my mouth, sweep the last bits with my chopsticks. I eat for Murasaki. I eat for Keiko.

I never thought I would end up in a hotel with a cowboy. I never expected to leave Japan. I never knew I would get married and then divorced. I never thought I would bear a daughter who speaks a different language. You never think. You never expect. You never know. But things still happen.

The *fubuki* has passed, and the clouds are tearing apart far enough so that the moon shows her face from time to time. When I was child in the house of my parents, when we were still rich with fatted land, we viewed the moon together and ate the special dumplings. Shige would sit on Okāsan's lap and I would sit on Otōsan's. And Okāsan would say,

"See, see how the rabbits are making *mochi* on the moon. They are taking turns pounding the rice."

But I never saw the rabbits on the moon. I only wished I could.

The tall buildings of downtown Calgary are mostly dim. Only a few squares of lights. Sometimes, a figure walks across, the light goes off and the room next to it is turned on. Someone is doing the night shift cleaning. Someone is always awake. The clouds have broken up the sky and the pale stars, dimmed by the orange street lights, wink off and on as the clouds silently drift. To Saskatchewan? I wonder. Tengu has fallen asleep with his hat on his head, his boots on his feet, and his coat buttoned up to his neck. He is so tired, he must be shouldering his own weight of stories untold and so back-breakingly heavy. I would at least tug his boots off his pinched feet, but I don't want to wake him up. It's better to just let him rest. So much could be done if we could just part with sleeping. If we didn't need to rest our heads from our daily cares. If only we could live in waking dreams, and not be clouded with the thin wisps of sleep and doubt. What magic we'd create around us. Instead of daily loaves of hate that we eat every morning and wash down with bitter coffee. *Che!* Stop it already! Enough of this depressing talk. You are born. If you are lucky, you live. And while you are alive, you might do a thing or two. Or not. It's up to that person, after all. After sitting in that chair in Keiko's house for twenty years, I guess I'm ready to do a thing or two. You can be old, but it doesn't mean you don't have a few tricks up your sleeve. Don't blink too slowly.

Murasaki

It was dark by the time I got home and Dad was asleep in front of the TV, a dirty plate with dried ketchup on the floor. I went upstairs to Mom's room and turned on the plug-in night light. Mom was still awake, or at least her eyes were still open, a plate of cold scrambled eggs on a tray in her lap. Ketchup on the side and two pieces of toast all congealed with a thin crust on top.

"Well, Obāchan is right. It's obvious you'll never get better on food like this and it looks pretty damn gross right now, doesn't it. Don't worry, Mom. Obāchan gave me some pointers and I met a woman named Sushi and Dad is a closet seaweed eater. Life is getting better."

Mom didn't move or blink, but I was feeling better and I knew she would too. I thumped downstairs and unloaded all my groceries. Dumped wieners and Cheese Whiz and left-over potato salad into the garbage. Carefully put away my store of treasure. I flicked on all the lights in the kitchen and turned on the radio. Honey murmur of a DJ soothing to my ears, I still sought the sound of voices in our hollow house. I sat down at the kitchen table and started to read my cookbook.

Tonkatsu (Deep fried breaded pork cutlets) *It's true.*

Bread crumbs all over the kitchen counters and crunching beneath my feet. I was red in the face and deep-frying pork chops for the first time in my life at eleven forty-five at night. Apparently, *Tonkatsu* is served with thinly sliced raw cabbage and I had three plates all ready, cabbage on the side. I couldn't stop putting a capital on the *t*, I couldn't stop thinking of it as our name. The deep-frying was a bad scene. I didn't know how done they were and took the first two out too soon, the outside fried, but the inside meat still pink and bleeding. Possible tapeworm fears. So I put them in the oil again, but I had waited too long and the bread crumb coating was too soggy so it all broke apart. I had to go outside, dump the oil on the gravel driveway, and start over again. The second time, I fried them too long and they came out harder than leather thongs. But it wasn't a wasted effort because, by then, I figured out that the *Tonkatsu* sank when they were raw and floated when they were done. What does this mean?

The third batch bobbed up light and golden, the pork just done and still tender. And while I was furiously cooking, bread crumbs flying in my wake, Dad was dreaming of something so close to his home he could almost taste it. He woke up in a daze and turned off the silent TV. He picked up his ketchup plate and set it in the sink. Washed all the dirty dishes I had made and wiped them and put them away. When I turned and finally noticed, he was sitting at the kitchen table, hands folded in his lap. He had set the table with forks and knives and the bottle of *Tonkatsu* sauce. There were three table settings. The *miso* soup I had made was overboiled and the seaweed was almost melted, but I served them up in bowls. Filled three more bowls with rice and a small plate with the pickled yellow *takuwan* that was little a strong in smell. I proudly placed my golden pork cutlets on the plates with sliced cabbage. One fifty-three in the morning. Funny, I thought, we're going to eat our name.

"Mom. Mom, supper's ready," I yelled up the stairs and crossed my fingers. Silence. Then a creak of floorboards. Slow, tentative steps, out the room, down the hall and down down the stairs. Mom, in Obāchan's *nemaki*, like a woman dreaming. A sleep walker. When Mom reached the bottom of the stairs, I held out my hand and she took it. We walked to the table together. Mom paused before she sat down and looked at the food before her.

"Where are the *hashi?*" she asked. "Chopsticks." Her voice creaky with disuse.

"We don't have any," I gently reminded. "We've never had any, Mom. We'll just have to use forks and knives, okay?"

"Wait a minute," Dad ran outside in his stocking feet,

even though it was snowing and he ran back in with twigs in his hands. A proud grin on his face. He plunked down on his seat and flicked out his Swiss Army knife. Started whittling, blading little knobs and scars off the twig in his hand until it was smooth. He flicked bark and bits of wood all over the kitchen floor, but Mom didn't say a thing, just waited until he had smoothed the second one and held out her hand. Dad gave her his home-made *ohashi* and she nodded her thanks. She raised her bowl of *miso* soup to her lips and slurped! *Zuru zuru zuru.* She slurped her soup and I was amazed. Dad kept on whittling and finished making two more sets of chopsticks.

"Oh, I got something for you too." I ran to the fridge and took out the small jar of salted seaweed paste. Opened the lid and set it in front of him.

"Thanks," he said and handed me my chopsticks. They felt awkward in my hands and I couldn't hold them. Couldn't bring food to my mouth. Dad didn't notice, he was heaping salted seaweed all over his bowl of rice with intense concentration. Mom looked up from her *miso* soup and saw. She took her fork and knife and cut my meat for me then poured *Tonkatsu* sauce evenly over my pork and a little over the cabbage. She took the chopsticks I was turning in my hands this way and that and held out my hand flat. Set the two thick ends of the chopsticks on my palm and closed my fingers over them in a fist. She turned my wrist ninety degrees and the points hung straight downward. Rigid and awkward, I could only make basic stabbing movements, which I did in the space above my plate. I looked up at Mom's face, wondering if she was making fun at me.

"Start eating. Like small child," her voice so thick and

dusty I couldn't recognize it. "Work from there."

I nodded slowly, beginning to understand. Something. I glanced at Dad, and he had cut his cutlet with his knife and fork too. He was holding his chopsticks with the grace and ease of a conductor, darting like swallows like fish. And Mom, the *ohashi* fit in her hands too. For all I had believed otherwise. I turned to my plate, my *hashi* in my fist, and stabbed a piece of meat with the points. I raised it to my nervous mouth and took a tentative bite. The bread crumbs crunchy and the pork tender firm, the sauce tangy and salty. It was good! I shoved the whole piece in my mouth and chewed with joy. Eating *Tonkatsu* in the heavy silence between night and dawn, a strange configuration.

There were no hugs or kisses or mea culpas. There wasn't a sudden wellspring of words, as if everything we never said burst forth and we forgave each other for all our shortcomings. We sat and ate. No one saying a word, just the smack of lips and tongues. We passed around the *Tonkatsu* sauce whenever it looked like someone was running out.

But it was a chrysalis time for Mom or me. Maybe for both of us, I don't know. Every day, we ate supper around midnight, food I had made from the Japanese cookbook and we used Dad's twig *ohashi*. Mom's words slowly coming back, or maybe me beginning to hear them. She didn't get up the next day and start cleaning the house or something like I had thought she would. She lay in bed all day and poked holes into the words she said out loud and laughed sometimes. It was nice hearing Mom laugh. I still stayed at home, to run the house and take the business calls. But mostly to hear the rich sound of my Mom's laughter.

(Murasaki: Obāchan.

Naoe: *Hai?*

Murasaki: Mom's feeling better now.

Naoe: Oh, I'm so glad to hear it.

Murasaki: And I'm cooking some Japanese food too.

Naoe: Murasaki. I'm glad. Do you like it?

Murasaki: Yes, I do. Obāchan?

Naoe: *Hai?*

Murasaki: Did you know that the sound of Mom's laughter makes you feel warm inside and all melty?

Naoe: I used to know.

Murasaki: I'm knowing now.

Naoe: Ask Keiko to clean your ears.

Murasaki: What?!

Naoe: Just ask her, Murasaki.

Murasaki: That's disgusting!

Naoe: Just ask.

Murasaki: Okay.)

"Mom," I asked, sitting on the corner of her bed, feeling slightly embarrassed but curious as well. "Could you clean my ears?" I was looking at her face, wondering what she would say or do. She looked bemused.

"You'll have to go look for the *mimikaki* in the bottom of your Obāchan's sewing box," she said, tying back the curtains in her room to let the sunlight in. I hopped up and went into Obāchan's room, the same as when she left. Her sewing box was on the homemade headboard shelf made out of two-by-fours. I sat on the bed and peered inside. Spools of thread and packets of shiny needles, a bag of unmatched buttons and scraps of yarn and cloth. Looking for the *mimikaki,* wondering what it was and if I would recognize it when I saw it. A long slender piece of wood, bamboo? and on one end, a tiny spoon head, and on the other, a fluffy ball of down, like a dandelion fluff Q-tip. Ahhhh, *mimikaki.* I went to Mom's room, and she was sitting up, a piece of Kleenex in her hand. She patted the bed and I sat down. She gently pulled my arm so I lay down, my head in her lap, the sun warm and cozy through the windowpane. Mom carefully tugged my ear lobe and cupped her other hand, her palm, beneath my chin, so the angle would be just right. The warm scent of Mom's clothes, seeping in the air. My eyes shut on their own accord and my body limped. Relaxed.

"My, you have quite a bit."

"Really?"

"It's a wonder you can hear anything at all."

"Really?" I wanted to look down my own ear, to see what was inside.

"Your ear channel goes straight down. Obāchan said

mine was quite twisty so she had a hard time cleaning them."

"Obāchan used to clean your ears?" I was amazed. It seemed like I was being amazed quite often, lately. Wondering what it meant.

"Oh, yes. She was really good at it too."

"Why didn't you or Obāchan ever clean my ears?"

"Did you ever ask?"

"No—"

"There you go," Mom said, "now no more talking, or I can't clean your ear. And don't move."

"Do it softly, Mom," I whispered. Closed my eyes to thought. And I felt the *mimikaki* dip inside my ear.

Anticipatory shudder of fear or longing or I don't know what. The thrill of bamboo piercing fragile tissue, tearing through tender flesh, but the longing for the first touch, the unknown. I hovered in that delicate place between anticipation and intense pleasure, teetering between fear and longing, hovered above the delicate skin over my closed eyes, a pinpoint of light yet heavy as golden honey. My trust lying in my mother's lap, my fragile skull, my legs curled up. Mom's clothes a warm breath around me, a cloud of bees, a palmful of seeds. Me and my heavy eyes shut and the sun stretched long beside me and time quivered like a taut skin. And soft soft softest scrape of bamboo scratching sensitive channel. The sensation was incredible. My mouth watered with delight, my toes curled in exquisite pleasure. The scrape scrape rustle so loud in my ear and the slow scratchy easing of tiny itches within. Mom softly lifted the *mimikaki,* tapped the wax on the Kleenex, and dipped the spoon again. Scrapes against skin never touched before but so softly itchy I never noticed until now, thrilling to the danger of bamboo piercing ear-drum yet the incredible unbearable pleasure.

"Does it hurt?"

"Don't stop," I say, the sun warm on my face, my body, the smell of her clothes, Mom scratch scratching so unbearably perfectly my teeth ache with the pleasure, a taste in my mouth like nectar.

It's funny how you never hear what you miss. After Mom cleaned my ears, I heard sounds I had never heard before. At least I didn't remember them. I walked around in wonderment, tilting my head from side to side, so the sounds could trickle into my ears more fully. I was bemused.

Apparently, the cicada has a long pupa stage. They live under the damp darkness of soil in silence for seven long years. Suck the juice from roots of trees and turn their blind underground eyes skyward, to dream of what they've never seen. For seven long years they churn in the ground their bodies white and tender, scrape their way through soil on two scythed arms, with serrated edges. After seven years of silence and darkness, they dig out from the soil and climb the bark of a tree. During the cover of night. In the morning there is nothing but a dry husk. The cicadas with newly patterned brittle wings fly off to other trees where they sit in the sun and shriek their songs, as long as there is light. They have only seven days to find a mate and complete their cycle so they shriek and hum and rattle and saw, with their bellows in their chest. They never shut up.

I have never seen a cicada. I have never heard them cry. What I know about them may be hearsay. It's a question of belief.

PART THREE

An Immigrant Story With a Happy Ending

Mukāshi, mukāshi, ōmukashi . . . . Nothing is impossible. Within reason, of course.

Part three. Everything that is missing or lost or caught between memory and make believe or forgotten or hidden or sliced from the body like an unwanted tumour.

Or

A longing, a desire for.

Forgetting or remembering something that never happened. Wondering when does one thing end and another begin? And if you can separate the two.

Part three.

The missing part.

PART FOUR

(Murasaki: Obāchan. Obāchan, help. Help me.

Naoe: *Ara,* what is it child?

Murasaki: Sometimes I'm so lonely I almost can't stand it. I get this ache here, and here, and I get this wobbly tremor in my throat and it makes me feel like I'll start crying and never stop again.

Naoe: Murasaki, it's the pain of growing up.

Murasaki: How can I be growing up still? I'm almost thirty.

Naoe: What then, you think some day you stop growing up? That's the day you die. The pain is hard, but it is important. You'll see.

Murasaki: I don't want to hear that now. All I can see is this awful pain inside.

Naoe: And you will be strong.

Murasaki: I can't.

Naoe: Yes, Murasaki.

Murasaki: I can't.

Naoe: Don't be *wagamama!* Do you think you are the only person who bears the ache of loneliness? Foolish child! You are a child still, if you think so.

Murasaki: Easy to be tough when you're ninety-seven. Two hundred and seven for all I know.

Naoe: Murasaki, it only gets harder and harder.

Murasaki: Then I might as well die.

Naoe: Yes, you might as well.

Murasaki: Obāchan!

Naoe: Do you want me to hold your hand forever? I wouldn't be doing you a favour. You stand on your own. *Warui koto yuwanai kara.*

Murasaki: How can I go on? Putting words in peoples' mouths. In yours, mine, distorting.

Naoe: *Che!* What, a sudden attack of conscience? I could be putting words in *your* mouth for all you know.

Murasaki: Really?

Naoe: Of course.

Murasaki: But I can't even come up with a new idea. A new story. It just turns over on itself, over and over again.

Naoe: Don't be vain. No one has a new idea. An infinite number of monkeys. And all that shit.

Murasaki: Obāchan! Where have you been picking up language like that?

Naoe: Murasaki, it has always been around. Why do you *amaeru* to me all the time? I don't want to coddle you forever.

Murasaki: Who else can I *amaeru* to?

Naoe: Your Mom, maybe?

Murasaki: You've got to be kidding!

Naoe: There are stranger things done beneath the midnight sun.

Murasaki: What! Are you in the Yukon?

Naoe: *Mattaku,* don't be so literal, Murasaki. I think we've exhausted this conversation!

Murasaki: All right, all right already.)

Murasaki

It was a strange winter of snow like fish scales. There wasn't a chinook the whole three months I stayed at home to care for Mom and I never ventured outside except to buy groceries. Once every two weeks, I sent Dad to Calgary with a list of items to buy at the Oriental Food Store. Sushi always sent back a box of strawberry-flavoured Pocky for me. On the house. I would eat the whole box of biscuit sticks dipped in strawberry chocolate while I watched "Ripley's Believe It Or Not" on TV.

Just me and Mom in the winter house of creaking walls and cobweb corners. I read books I found in the attic from the last people who lived in it. Actually, the house wasn't always here. It was originally built in High River and someone had had the whole creaking mess hauled on a flatbed truck in the middle of the night. The belly of the house getting so much stress that they couldn't squeeze it back together again. Fractures and wrinkles all over the house so the wind never stopped blowing through. There were books in the attic, and sometimes strange photos would fall out of the walls when the wind shook them too hard.

It wasn't like we were suddenly best friends. It wasn't that we forgot everything unsaid. Those three months were a neutral zone and we could talk of quiet things out loud.

"Mom," I was sitting on her bed, leaning against the headboard. She sat in front of me and I was brushing her hair.

"Yes?" she said dreamily. Her body weaving with every stroke of the brush.

"What does Murasaki mean?"

Mom stopped weaving and opened her eyes.

"Purple." She started swaying again.

Purple, I thought. Purple as thought as mood as amethyst, yuck! As blood as eggplant as grapes so swollen round puurrrrrple. Hmmmmm.

"Why do you suppose Obāchan called me purple?"

"I don't know. Could be a number of reasons."

"So what would your guess be?" I asked softly, so she wouldn't end the conversation.

"Please don't stop brushing."

"Oh, sorry. So can you tell me what she might have meant?"

"Well, it might be her favourite colour."

"Oh." Disappointed. "That's all, huh."

"Or. . . ."

"Or what?"

"Well, there was a woman named Murasaki Shikibu born in the late tenth century Japan."

"This sounds more promising."

"She is the first person to write a novel. As far as we know," Mom amended. "Well, not a novel in the Western sense, because it was written on scrolls but she was the first person to write a long piece of prose that was in fact a story and not just a diary thing or some sort of lesson."

"Wow, that's cool."

"And not only that," Mom continued, warming to the subject, "she is considered to be the first person ever to create the antihero."

"Wow. Have you read the book?"

"A long time ago."

"What's it called?"

"Genji Monogatari."

"What does that mean?"

"Roughly, *The Tale of Genji.*"

"What's it about?"

"You're full of questions, aren't you."

"Well, I want to get as many in as I can, in case you stop answering," I say, brushing her hair with long even strokes.

"That's practical. *Genji Monogatari* is about a nobleman named Genji and his life at court and his various adventures with ladies."

"Oh." Disappointed again. "Kinda like an anchored royal Love Boat with a Hirohito Tom Jones?"

"The things you come up with! Don't make judgements until you've read it, Muriel. Actually, if you can read beneath the surface, it gives an aching account of what life was like for women of court in the eleventh century."

"Sorry. I wonder if they'll have it in the Nanton library?"

"Maybe try the university."

"I think I will. Thanks. Is there anything special you want for supper?"

"Mmmmm. Anything you make is fine, Muriel."

• • •

She thumped down the stairs, the rug flat and hard where everyone placed their feet. Her grandmother's chair still in the hall. More than a wooden presence. It wasn't contoured with carved swirling arms, or curved for the body. It had a flat back with no ornamentation and no armrests to offer meager comfort. A simple chair with only a hint of a concave the old woman's buttocks had worn away over two decades of perseverance. The chair was in an awkward position so it was even a greater disturbance to walk around because there was no one sitting in it. The young woman reached out to touch the seat of the chair, but pulled back her hand before contact. Shivered. Stepped carefully around it and into the kitchen. The wind slid through the space between floor and wall, minute cracks around the window frames. She checked the clock above the sink, five thirty-six. It was already dark outside. She crossed her bare arms and vigorously rubbed her icy skin with her hands, briskly, up and down, but it only made the surface warmer for an instant, then was snatched away with a sudden gust that made the windows rattle. Too early to start supper, too late to start a book, she decided to watch the news for half an hour.

From the living room, she could see three of the four walls of the house, and the windows and the view they offered. She bent down to switch on the television, when something swirled on the edge of her sight, just outside the living room window. She whirled around, but the movement stayed beyond her focus. The girl felt something whisk by again, and she twisted to just miss something swirl past the dining room. She spun from window, to window, to catch the movement with her eyes, but it whirled on and on, circling the house in dizzy spirals, the girl spinning and spinning, always one turn too slow to ever see. The ground tipping and sliding beneath her feet, her eyes watered with nausea. She stumbled to the hall, was drawn to her Obāchan's chair. The only steady object in the heaving of the house. The floorboards lurched beneath her feet, the walls stretched then waned, a kettle, a toaster, the vacuum cleaner spinning in the air. Dead bodies of moths spiralled off the floor to mimic a patterned flight. She reached for the back of the chair with a shaking hand. With a single touch, everything was still. The toaster, back on the kitchen counter, the kettle on the stove. The vacuum cleaner nestled in the bottom of the closet. Dead moths heaped in the corners of the hallway. The girl turned jerkily, the backs of her knees bumping the seat of the chair, her heart beating so loudly it scattered her breath in her chest. She took a long shuddering gasp of air and held it in her lungs. Sat down with dread and longing.

She felt her body mold into the shape, the contour of the chair. Her legs shrinking to swing above the floor, her fingers curling into bulging bone. Her buttocks curved into the hollow carved out of the seat. "This chair feels just right," she whispered, in a Goldilock's voice. She sat in the cold hallway and wasn't troubled with any thoughts. Just sat and watched the seeping wind pattern dust on the icy floorboards. Sat for moments or decades without knowing or even caring.

Looked up with a start. Her silent mother, looming in the darkness. She stood at the top of the stairway, so dark the girl couldn't make out her eyes, her lips. Only the cotton pale gleam of her grandmother's *nemaki.*

"Obāchan, you'll ruin your eyes, sitting in the dark like this. If you're going to insist on sitting in the hall, at least turn on the lights. Really, I wish you'd have more sense!"

"Denki nanka iranai yo. Yokei na osewa," the young woman said, and shuddered. The hair standing on her arms and neck, shuddered so hard that she could feel pee trickling down her thigh. Her mother just sighed noisily and thumped back to her bedroom. The girl sat in the chair without moving.

• • •

"You mean your Obāchan took over your body?" you ask.

"No, that's not it at all. It wasn't a thing of taking over—more of a coming together. Or a returning. I don't know. I might even be making this all up as I go along." I impatiently scrounge through the deep freeze for my emergency package of cigarettes.

"What are you looking for?"

"A package of smokes. I know I had a pack of smokes in here."

"Anoneeee," you say, scratching the back of your head in embarrassment, "I might have smoked them last Sunday when you were out."

I spin around. "What do you mean, 'I might have.'? You did or you didn't. Unless you've put some in yourself and smoked your own." You shake your head.

"Jesus," I sigh, roll my eyes. "It's too bloody cold out to get in the car let alone drive to the store."

"You want me to go get you some?"

"Nah, I'm not that bad. Maybe I'll bake some cookies or something. I feel a bit restless."

"Because of your ghost story?" you ask, opening eyes wide in fear or skepticism.

"It's doesn't have to be a ghost story. Unless you think it is. It's a question of belief."

Naoe

Ahhh, nothing like a nice tub full of steaming water. You can't take a proper bath unless the water is so hot you have to tease yourself into it, one toe at a time. So hot, the water, your skin feels like pins and needles, all prickly and itchy. If you scratch the surface of your skin, big fat red welts plump up in the heat. Funny how one language has words for some things and not words for others. Water, I can say, and who is to know if I mean hot or cold. Funny limits to what I say and what is understood. *Mizu,* I'll say, and I'll get a cold glass of water, maybe pulled up from a well in a bucket on the end of a long wet rope. *Oyu,* I'll say, and someone will surely fill the tub with steaming hot water. Yes, limits to sounds and utterances, always something misconstrued. Water, I'll say, and I never know what I'll get.

Funny how you can live so long and not have a new idea for years at a time. Finding yourself measuring the time past by how old your child begins to look. And still so much to do. Surely, time can be spent wondering what will be eaten for supper, but after that meal is in the belly, where will people turn their thoughts to? So smug in the order of animals. We are the top of the animal kingdom, no! We are superior to the animal kingdom because we are capable of thinking. *Che!* Who can know when the last human being had a thought, superior or otherwise?

No one thinks they aren't thinking. Such foolish vain selfish creatures we are. And I'm not one to fool myself. I can be lulled by a plate full of creamy lobster, a tub full of hot *oyu.* Redundant usage.

(Naoe: Murasaki-chan?

Murasaki: *Hai?*

Naoe: My, such a quick *henji!*

Murasaki: I've decided it wouldn't do me any harm to be polite sometimes.

Naoe: So you have been talking with your mother?

Murasaki: *Hai.*

Naoe: And you had your ears cleaned?

Murasaki: *Hai.*

Naoe: I'm glad. A daughter should be close enough to have her ears cleaned by her mother.

Murasaki: That would gross out a lot of people, you know.

Naoe: I suppose it's culturally specific.

Murasaki: Not to mention appal a few doctors.

Naoe: Well, you can't please everyone.

Murasaki: So I'm finding.

Naoe: Murasaki-chan?

Murasaki: *Hai?*

Naoe: I want to hear you tell a story.

Murasaki: What? I can't tell a story. Out loud. I wouldn't even know where to begin. You're supposed to be the one telling stories to me. You know, the grandmother telling stories of the past to the avidly listening grandchild and all that.

Naoe: Have you listened to me? Have you heard my stories?

Murasaki: *Hai.*

Naoe: And you enjoyed them?

Murasaki: *Hai.*

Naoe: And don't you think stories are shared. That there is a partnership in the telling and listening, that it is of equal importance?

Murasaki: Well, if you put it that way, I suppose you're right.

Naoe: Murasaki-chan, we have only come part way in the telling and the listening. We must both be able to tell. We must both be able to listen. If the positions become static, there can never be stories. Stories grow out of stories grow out of stories. Listening becomes telling, telling listening.

Murasaki: *Ehhhhhh.*

Naoe: So come, tell me a wonderful story. I am sitting in a hot bath, up to my neck in silky heat. A story now will rush to my head and make it spin like no *sake,* no *shōchū.*

Murasaki: What's *shōchū?*

Naoe: Always asking questions. That's a good way of learning things, but I'm still waiting.

Murasaki: Okay, already. Here goes, but promise not to laugh.

Naoe: I promise.)

Mukāshi, mukāshi, ōmukashi . . .

(Murasaki: Obāchan?

Naoe: *Hai?*

Murasaki: I don't think I'm ready.

Naoe: Oh. When will you be ready, child?

Murasaki: Soon. Very soon. But promise you'll be with me when I start. It's very frightening and what if I get stuck or something?

Naoe: Trust me. I'll be there. And if you falter, I will fill in the words for you until you are ready again.

Murasaki: Can we do that?

Naoe: Murasaki-chan, we can do almost anything.)

"Funny thing, that. You call your *mago*, Murasaki, and tell me to call you Purple. Why do you suppose?" Tengu asks, cupping lukewarm water in his palms and letting it slide down the bones of my spine.

"Ara! When did you come in? I didn't even notice you getting in the tub!"

"I heard you talking and I wanted to listen," he says, glances at my eyes. "I hope I haven't offended you or anything."

"Ehhh, well I guess it's all right. You listened so quietly, I didn't even hear you."

"So, who is Murasaki and who is Purple?"

"The words are different, but in translation, they come together."

"So you're a translation of Murasaki and Murasaki is a translation of you?" Tengu touches my back with a fingertip, his palm, stroking downward. I lean slowly back.

"That's one reading of it," I say. My eyes are sleepy, but my skin is warming inside the cooling water.

"Is there more than one?" he whispers.

"Always."

"Do you want to fuck?"

"Let me translate the answer with my body."

Murasaki

It's an easy thing to hate your mother when you are eleven and living in what you can only see as agricultural hell. It was a time when I came to realize that the shape of my face, my eyes, the colour of my hair affected how people treated me. I never felt different until I saw the look crossing peoples' faces. I don't know if it's better to come to realize, or not realize at all. When I didn't know, I was happily innocent. When I finally noticed, the measure of my discontent knew no boundaries. Old Richard Third wasn't the only one in the winter of his life.

Mom knew from the start. She knew from the start but all she chose to do was hide beneath a fluffy woolly skin of a white sheep. This was her only safety. She chose the great Canadian melting pot and I had to live with what she ladled.

I thumped up the porch, two steps at a time, and slammed the screen door open, tumbling inside.

"Ara!" Obāchan said. *"Dōshitano?"*

She was sitting in her chair, like always. Our sentinel. Our protectress. Such an uncomfortable wooden chair, and she never used a cushion. Her feet dangling above the floor. No windows to see outside, just the small pane of peel-and-stick plastic "stained glass" in the diamond-shaped frame in the door. Too high up to see out of. I sat carefully in her lap and put my arms around her thin neck. She smiled up at me and stroked my long straight hair.

"Guess what, Obāchan? I've been given the lead in our school operetta! I get to play the part of Alice in Wonderland and I have tons and tons of lines to memorize, but isn't it great? I got the lead!"

"Iikocha!" She cupped her scratchy palm beneath my

chin, her fingers curving along my cheek. I kissed her. Jumped up and ran into the kitchen.

"Mom! Mom! Guess what!"

"What, Muriel? I wish you wouldn't slam the door."

"I've been chosen to play the part of Alice in the school operetta!"

"Oh how wonderful!" Mom looked up from the accounts she had been doing and pushed her glasses up with her forefinger. She patted my shoulder awkwardly. "I'm so proud of you. You have such a lovely voice and now everyone will hear you sing. I have to call your father."

"There's a meeting for the moms tomorrow after school, okay?" I nibbled a piece of my hair.

"Of course, dear," Mom said. "I'll be right on time."

Mom came right on time, with her going-out purse and pumps. She had done her hair in rollers, and the fat curls made her head look two times bigger than it really was. Her eyebrows were newly plucked and penciled in darker than the original colour.

"So good of you to come, Mrs. Ton Kasu. We are so proud of our little Muriel. Such a lovely singing voice, who would have thought?" Mrs. Spear beamed at my Mom. She tugged my Mom's elbow and drew her to the side. She looked sideways, this and that, with the whites of her eyes, rolling, and lowered her voice into a whisper. I edged in closer.

"There is a matter of delicacy I want to speak to you about."

"Of course," Mom said, smiling.

"Well, it's the matter of your daughter's hair. You see, the part she is playing, you know the story of Alice in Wonderland, don't you?"

Mom shook her head apologetically.

"Well, Alice is a story about an English girl, you know. An English girl with lovely blonde hair. And strictly for the play, you understand, Muriel will have to have blonde hair or no one will know what part she is playing. You simply cannot have an Alice with black hair."

"Of course," Mom nodded, to my growing horror. "It's in the nature of theatre and costume, is it not?"

"Of course!" Mrs. Spear beamed. "I knew you would understand. I was thinking of a nice blonde wig. They make such nice wigs these days, no one will notice a thing. Why, they'll think there's a new child in school who is star material! You must be so proud."

"We could dye her hair. I believe there are dyes that wash out in a few months or so. That way, Muriel can really grow into her role as Alice. She can live and be Alice before opening night!"

"Mrs. Ton Kasu! You are so cooperative. I wish my other mothers were more like you. Why I was just telling Mrs. Rogowski her daughter should lose at least ten pounds before the play, and she just up and left in a tiff. Pulling her daughter after her. Poor dear, when she was so looking forward to being in the play."

I was horrified, Mom and Mrs. Spear chatting away and dye my beautiful black hair blonde? Me with blonde hair and living the role of Alice? In Nanton? What could my Mom be thinking? I would look ridiculous and stand out like a freak.

"Mom!" I hissed. "Mom, I changed my mind. I don't want to be Alice anymore. I'll be the Mad Hatter, that way, I can just wear a hat. Or the Cheshire Cat! Cats have slanted eyes. That would work out. Mom?"

She just ignored me and chatted with Mrs. Spear, about costume and hair dyes and suitable diets for actors. On the way home from school she stopped at the drugstore and dragged me inside. To discuss the merits of hair rinse over henna with Mrs. Potts.

We had baked ham for dinner that night, because Mom was so proud of me. Dad just smiled and poured me a small glass of sherry. It was sticky and cloyingly sweet. I nodded and sipped and ate dry slices of meat with burnt pineapple rings. Obāchan in her chair by the door, her voice as constant as the wind. She would stick her head out now and then, and wink and smile at me from the other end of the hall. Mom and Dad didn't notice her or pretended not to. They ate their chunks of burnt special-occasion ham and blackened pineapple garnish.

She never sat at the table with us, we never ate together. Obāchan had a tray of food brought upstairs for her to eat in bed. Long after we had finished our Jell-O and weak milk tea. But she hardly ever ate what Mom had cooked for her. Obāchan ate treats she had hidden in her dresser drawers and threw the dry meat out the window for the coyotes who waited every evening.

Mom excused me from washing dishes, just for this one time. I went upstairs, saying something about a headache, and heard Mom telling Dad it was because I was so excited. I went inside my room and didn't turn on the lights. Lay down on my bed and watched the growing shadows creeping across the ceiling.

I shivered awake, the room all black and I didn't know if it was today or tomorrow. I was lying on my bed with all my clothes on and the house was silent. Creaking. And I noticed it. A warm wetness beneath my bum. Oh god. . . I had wet my pants! I had peed my pants! I jumped up and flicked on the light. My powder blue blanket was stained all copper brown. Diarrhea? Shit my pants? What? Oh my god… it was blood. I was haemorrhaging. Dying. Bleeding to death. I unbuttoned my jeans and slid down the zipper. Thumbed my panties down with my jeans and stared. There was lots of blood. Certainly, it was too much blood. I didn't know I was whimpering, standing there with blood plipping between my legs.

"Murasaki-chan? Dōshita! Sonna koe dashite?"

"Obāchan! Obāchan, I'm bleeding to death. Call Mom or the ambulance or something." Started gulping back tears.

"Dore, misetegoran," and she crouched beside me. I was frightened and didn't want her to see, but she saw my bloody panties, the blanket on my bed.

"Yokatta! Yappari. Shinpai iranai yo. Tsuki no mono ga hajimattan da yo. Onna ni daijina, daijina koto yo." She smiled gently, warmly, and I knew everything was all right.

"Oh," I smiled through my tears. "Is that all."

"Sōyū koto!" Obāchan took a clean pair of underwear out of my dresser and led me to the washroom. She helped me out of my bloody ones and set them in the sink. She rummaged in the cupboard and came out with a rectangular white paper wad. There was an adhesive strip down the middle covered with a strip of paper. She tugged it off and stuck the bandage in the crotch of my panties.

"Oh," I said. And put them on. Obāchan turned on the tap, adjusting the hot and cold, once twice, three times, checking the temperature on the inside of her wrist. She gently took my hand and held my wrist beneath the flow of water. The temperature was so nearly that of my body I couldn't tell if it was warm or cool. Only the sensation of water running on my wrist. Obāchan held the panties under the stream and the blood washed from the cloth like magic.

Only a faint stain was left. She wrung it out and tossed it in the laundry hamper.

"Oide!" and took my hand again. I felt happy, I don't know why.

"Obāchan, what's going on out there? We're trying to get some sleep you know. Have a little consideration!" Mom yelled from her room. Dad groaned, only waking up because she had been yelling across his head.

Obāchan and I, we giggled as we went into her bedroom. She hadn't been asleep at all, her lights were on and there was silky paper with characters written in black ink.

"Whatchya writing, Obāchan? A letter or something?" I asked wistfully. Wishing that seeing was the same as reading. She shook her head and started digging in her closet where she had a huge pile of boxes stacked one on top of another. Pointed to one in the middle and gestured for me to get it out.

"Sure, no problem," I muttered. "Mom's going to have a conniption fit, whatever that is, if these boxes start falling down." But I managed to get it down with little noise and opened up the four flaps. Obāchan hunkered beside me and lifted out Japanese newspapers, magazines, a few smaller boxes, and a cloth bag with something in it. She took the smallest box, covered in patterned paper, and the little sack tied with string. Lifted the lid of the box and I peered inside, thinking of jewels and treasures. There was nothing inside except some beans. A burgundy-ish reddish bean with a small mark where the root would eventually come out. Then, she opened the cloth sack, folding the top back on itself so I could see inside. Roundish white seeds lay inside.

"Beans, huh," I stuck my finger in the box to stir them around. "And rice. That's nice, Obāchan."

"Tada no mame to kome janai yo," she said sternly.

"Sorry."

She led me downstairs, the wood creak creaking beneath our feet and we shushed each other and giggled. Obāchan took the beans and soaked them in a bowl of tepid water. She held up two fingers.

"They have to soak for two hours, huh."

I went upstairs to get my blankets and took them down to the large sink in the laundry room. Checking the temperature of the water on my wrist once, twice, three times to make sure it was the same as my body's. The blood ran red into the water, making it a pretty pink. I hummed as I washed, until Mom stomped on the floor with her heel from her bedroom above. I could hear Dad moaning through the floorboards. I wrung out the blankets and hung them over the washer and dryer, puddles starting to form.

Obāchan sat at the kitchen table. She was sorting through the seeds of rice, picking out any that were slightly black or broken. I sat beside her and helped. I must have fallen asleep, and only woke up because there was a rich steamy fragrance in the air that I had never smelled before. Obāchan stood at the stove, filling two bowls with something from a pot. I went to the washroom and tidied my hair. Washed my face with icy water. When I came back, Obāchan was already sitting at the table, two bowls of rice in front of her. But the rice was different. It wasn't white, but a rich purpley reddish colour and there were bean flecks here and there.

"Omedetō," Obāchan reached, cupped my cheek, my chin, in the palm of her scratchy hand.

"Thank you," I said, and bowed my head. Picked up my bowl of rice.

"Sekihan," you say. "You eat it for other special occasions too."

"Oh," I am a little disappointed. I wanted it for women only.

"I can make it."

"Really?" Beginning to perk up. "I would love to have some."

"What will we celebrate?" you ask.

"Don't worry. I'll think of something."

"What do you want to do while we soak the beans for two hours?"

"You have to ask?"

He taught flower arranging and the art of the Japanese tea ceremony for Calgary Continuing Education. His students were mostly women who could only take classes in the evenings. He didn't make enough money doing this, so he worked as a night watchperson for extra pay. I delivered pre-dawn newspapers and we'd lie together when the days were bright and glowing.

I circled my finger on his smooth belly, tickled his feet with my toes. He was all sleepy and warm and the sun a fine thin comforter.

"I'd like to speak with your Obāchan sometime," he said drowsily.

"You are. . . ."

But he was asleep.

"This is great," I muffled, through sweet purple rice. "It's almost as good as what Obāchan made for me, that one time."

"So what are we celebrating?" he asked, scooping up another bowlful of *sekihan.*

"A love story."

"Nani?"

"A love story. This love story right now. I'm not embarrassed. I decided that we could be a love story and be very proud about it," I was feeling smug about my discovery. Of voicing it out loud.

"Does this mean we will be married?" he asked, serious.

"Of course not. 'Love story' and 'marriage' side by side would be an oxymoron. Why not linger in a love story? You would hate being married to me." I confided, carefully trying to pick out some beans from my rice. Avoiding his face.

"My parents are coming to meet you in the fall," he said, watching my eyes.

"Why?"

"Because, we've been living together. Because I write letters about you. Because they think we should get married and I think they're right." He was serious.

"Is this a proposal?" I asked, sad, angry, pleased all at the same time that my thoughts were jumbled and I couldn't choose my words with care.

"Murasaki, I didn't think I needed to ask. I thought this was a partnership for life."

"Like Canada geese, huh? Like Mandarin ducks."

"I'm not joking," he said. He was getting angry, and I couldn't blame him.

"I'm not either." I stood up. Clattered my empty bowl in the sink.

"Then why are you here, why are you here right now, eating my rice and sleeping with me during the day?"

"Because I want to. And you want me to."

"I just want you to commit yourself to us," he said. "That's what people do when they love each other, isn't it?"

"I am committed to us."

"Than prove it."

"I'm committed to us at this moment. Right now. But if you keep bugging me about it, I might change my mind."

"How can I trust you if you can't make a commitment? This is a once in a lifetime relationship. It doesn't get any better than this. We could live in a thousand lifetimes and never find something so special again. What more are you waiting for?"

"I'm not waiting for another lover, if that's what you're worried about. I just can't commit my whole *life* to you.

Especially if I don't know what might happen next. If something bigger than just us comes into our lives."

"But you do that every day," he said, frustrated with my inconsistencies. "You commit yourself to what you don't know every time you tell a story."

"I'm committed to this love story right now. Can't that be enough?"

"Everything you think of, you have to interpret as story. I'm not just a story. You're not just a story. We feel and think and age and learn. If you hit me, it will hurt. If you leave me, I will cry. You can't just erase those things."

"I'm not erasing. I'm re-telling and re-creating." I stood at the window, looking outside at the mugo pine you have been trying to shape.

"There's no talking to you when you're like this. You're the hardest person I've ever loved."

"Past tense?"

"I have to go out," and he didn't smile.

"Hey," you say, "you're mixing up the story with what's really happening right now in our lives. I don't know if I like that. I want to be able to separate the stories from our real lives. What we're living right now." You wash out the bowls, the rice cooker and hashi. You are anxious and the dishes clatter noisier than when you are content.

"You can't. The words give the shape to what will happen. What can happen. I'm telling our future before it ever does." I wander into the living room, touch the back of the couch, thumb a row of books, run a finger through the dust on top of the black stereo.

"But what if I don't like the future you shape for us? What about my say in our future?" You are wiping your hands on a towel and your hair is tousled from frustrated fingers.

"When I'm finished my story, you can start another if you want. I will listen as politely as you have listened. At least, I'll try to," I amend.

"I don't know if we should be messing around with our future. It might be unlucky," you say earnestly.

"Luck has nothing to do with it. Well, maybe a little bit, but mostly, we hold the power to change our lives for ourselves. I don't want to rely on fate."

"What if—"

I put a finger to your lips and pull you to the floor. Rest your head in my lap and stroke your hair, the lovely lines in your widow's peak.

"Trust me."

I wiped the dishes he left sitting in the draining rack and sat in front of the TV, even though it wasn't on. Thoughts of gift horses and teeth and Mandarin ducks. Whatever they were. Funny how loving and pain are so closely tied together. When I was younger, I would have died to have thought I could find a man with a widow's peak who could cook and love me with commitment. Me, who loved happy endings, despite myself. *Henkutsu.* The word lingered. Obstinately contrary. No, it wasn't just that, though I couldn't think of a word that described me better. Something tugged at my heart, my soul, that kept me from staying forever. Obāchan here. Obāchan now. Obāchan then and always.

"Tadaima," he said, sounding tired. I was still sitting on the couch.

"Hi. How were your classes?"

"All right. I have a few students who show some promise. What are you doing?" He dropped down on the couch beside me. The bitter-green scent of flower stems seeping from his clothes and hands.

"Nothing. Thinking"

"What were you thinking?"

"It occurred to me. That I've known you since you arrived at the airport, but you've never taken an English class at the Y or anything. And you're so fluent, I don't even notice an accent when we're talking together."

He looked incredulously at me.

"But when I speak with you, I only speak in Japanese. *Jibun de wakaranai no? Itsumo Nihongo de hanashiteiru noni."* 呆れるよ。

Oh.

• • •

He leaned back, his head against the rim of the bathtub, and closed his eyes. She lingered, curling her fingers around his toes, and stroked the bottom of his feet with strong hands. He sighed. She circled his ankles, cupped the back of his calves with her palms, her knees tucked beneath her, straddling his feet. Smoothed hands slick with soap, up the back of his calves, circled his knees, along his thighs. She kneaded his legs with her powerful hands and he felt the tension seeping from his body. The breath hissed between his parted lips. She ran one finger up the skin of his inner thigh, stroked tender-smooth. He moaned. She smiled, and stretched a sure hand. Touch. The soft skin of a salamander. He sucked back his breath and held, sighed with dismay when she moved her hand away. Stretched her hand again. Touch. Touch. Salamander smooth. He held his breath. She lipped the skin of his belly, tongue stroking, bit softly his tiny nipples. Kissed him softly on his brow, his cheek, his eyes. She lifted her pelvis with a small motion, warm water lapping, the moisture in her hair, streaming down her face, breasts, moved her pelvis over him and tucked him deep inside. They rocked, slowly and gently, the water lapping around her thighs, his belly, they rocked and slid and he arched his back and she pressed, she pressed and hisssss of breath released. She laughed.

• • •

THE HERALD
The Multicultural Voices of Alberta, Part 4: Japanese Canadians Today

My name is Keiko, but please call me Kay. I've lived in Alberta for twenty years and like it very much.

Nothing seems more fragile yet symbolic of resilient life as the wild crocus blooming every spring despite a covering of ice and snow. I would never move to Vancouver to retire. There are too many Japanese there who wish they were in Japan. I could never understand why those people ever left if they always pine for the past.

When I decided to immigrate, I decided to be at home in my new country. You can't be everything at once. It is too confusing for a child to juggle two cultures. Two sets of ideals. If you want a child to have a normal and accepted lifestyle, you have to live like everyone else. This has nothing to do with shame in one's own culture, but about being sensible and realistic. If you live in Canada, you should live like a Canadian and that's how I raised my own daughter. It's very simple, really.

That's my advice to new immigrants. I've had a happy and easy life here, and I would never want to live anywhere else. This is my home. These are my neighbours.

• • •

My name is Murasaki. My mother calls me Muriel, but I out-grew that name when I came to realize that I came from a specific cultural background that wasn't Occidental. Whatever that means.

I was born in High River, but I grew up in Nanton, a small rural town south of Calgary. Life is hard in Canada, once you come to an age when you find out that people think certain things of you just because your hair is black and they have watched "Shogun, the Mini Series." I had a grandmother who could only speak Japanese, but I never spoke with her because I never learned the language. I wasn't given the chance to choose.

I feel a lot of bitterness about how I was raised, how I was taught to behave. I had a lot of questions about my heritage, but they were never answered. The place where we lived didn't foster cultural difference. It only had room for cultural integration. If you didn't abide by the unwritten rules of conduct, you were alienated as an other, subject to suspicion and mistrust.

It was easy when I was an innocent. I could swallow everything I was told. I'm not finished asking questions and I never will be. Home should be a safe place, but there are times when I don't feel safe at all.

And I have to wonder where I live.

• • •

Kiyokawa Naoe wa iru. Mukashi mo ita. Korekara nochi mo iru. Canada wa hiroi. Jitto mimi o sumashite kiite goran, ironna koe ga kikoeru kara. Kokoro no-mimi o mottetara ne. Do you know your neighbour? Do you even want to? Will you ever? If you leave your home and start walking this road, I'll meet you somewhere.

• • •

Murasaki

Mom got better. She ate food and I brushed her hair and sometimes, when I felt lonely, I asked her to clean my ears. One day, she got out of bed and took off Obāchan's *nemaki*. Folded it up and put it away in Obāchan's dresser drawer. She put on her own slacks and blouse and curled her hair in fat rollers. She plucked her eyebrows and pencilled them in darker than the original colour. I just watched her, bustling around, feeling a little sad.

"Do you feel better, Mom?"

"Yes, I feel much better. Thank you, Muriel." And that was that. We didn't talk about Obāchan leaving, or why they wouldn't talk together. Why they only talked apart. We didn't talk about why Mom was sick for three months and why she left important things behind her when they left Japan. I never thought we would have a happy ending, Mom and I, but I was still sad when it was time for her to get well again. Funny how she had to be sick for us to be able to come to a place where we could have some contact. Maybe, I thought, maybe I can get sick next time.

Mom got better and I went back to school. She still cooked her lasagna and roast chicken, her blocks of beef, but sometimes, on a holiday weekend, she would ask me to whip up something from "my little cook book," as she called it. And I knew.

"I'm sorry," he said, "I hope I didn't put you off. I guess I'm still a little old-fashioned." We were lying side by side in the middle of the giant *futon.* He snuggled his arms around my waist from behind. Nestling his face in the fold of my neck.

"Me too."

"You're old-fashioned too?" he said, sounding hopeful.

"No, I mean I'm sorry. Though I may be at that. I never really thought about it. I suppose I'm old-fashioned about some things, but not about the marriage thing. That doesn't mean I'm messing around, but the institution of marriage isn't my idea of what a commitment is about. I could be committed to you from ten thousand miles away, you know."

"Are you planning on going somewhere?"

"The idea's been on my mind lately."

"Oh."

He rolled on to his back and he looked up at the ceiling. Looked up at dusty thread of cobweb, weaving back and forth, back and forth, in the unseen movement of air. I slid my hands back through his lovely widow's peak. Followed the bones of his face to cup his jaw in my palm. There were tears in his eyes. I leaned down to kiss his cheek, his brow, his eye, tasted his sadness on my tongue. I reached down and tucked him deep inside me. We rocked and rocked, slowly, gently, the strand of thread weaving in the air above us.

You decide to leave, go on a journey, and people will say this and that. They want to tag you with something so that questions are neatly answered. A reason for everything around them. She's troubled, she's searching for something. Or she's running away. Not taking it at face value. How to measure the cost?

The journey begins inside my head. With thoughts and words like my Obāchan before me. And when I'm gone, after I'm gone, I'll send post cards now and then, so people won't have to worry.

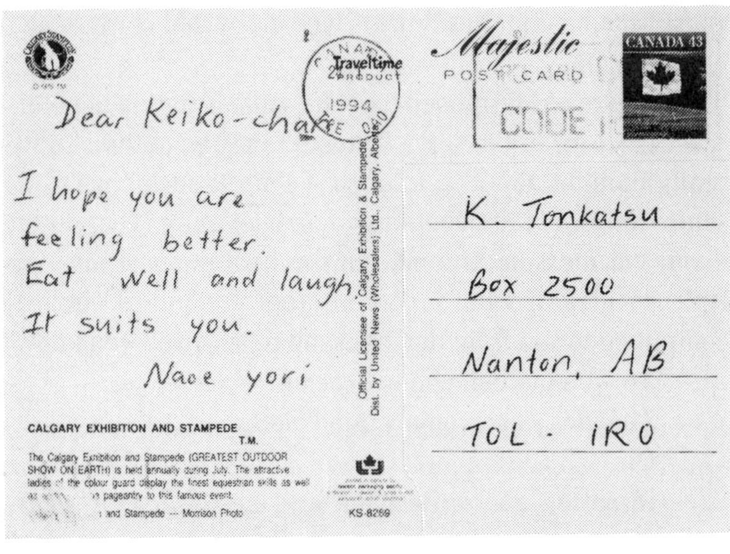

Majestic
POST CARD
CANADA 43
Traveltime PRODUCT
1994

Dear Keiko-chan

I hope you are
feeling better.
Eat well and laugh
It suits you.

Naoe yori

K. Tonkatsu
Box 2500
Nanton, AB
TOL · IRO

Official Licensee of Calgary Exhibition & Stampede
Dist. by United News (Wholesalers) Ltd., Calgary, Alberta

CALGARY EXHIBITION AND STAMPEDE T.M.

The Calgary Exhibition and Stampede (GREATEST OUTDOOR SHOW ON EARTH) is held annually during July. The attractive ladies of the colour guard display the finest equestrian skills as well as [illegible] pageantry to this famous event.

[illegible] and Stampede — Morrison Photo

KS-8269

• • •

"I shouldn't call you Tengu. You should tell me what you want me to call you. It was presumptuous of me," she said, her arm across his chest. She ran her bath-wrinkled fingers over the smoothness of his belly. He reached over to the night stand and tapped a Mild Seven out of a crumpled pack. Turned to her and raised his eyebrows. She took it and tucked it above her ear. He tapped out another and lit it with the hotel matches. Hotel Regis.

"When I was little, my dad was a ranch hand, a foreman, and we lived out west, in the foothills. He'd wake up before dawn and bloody cold out, so early in the morning and fresh out of bed, and haul feed to the bulls and drive a few of those huge round bales of hay out to the far pasture and milk the cows and check the coop for some fresh warm eggs, blue ones, we had guinea hens, and kick the old turkey for hissing too closely and be back inside after a good three hours of solid work, the sun wouldn't even be peeping over the low scrub of the foothills. He'd come back inside, his flesh all chilled and press his cold nose in my neck and I'd squeal and run into his girlfriend's and his bedroom and snuggle beside her and she'd stick her head out over the covers, she liked to sleep with her head beneath them, and say, You done the chores? Yup, he'd say, and toss me up in the air and let me fall to the bed and I'd laugh and laugh. Come on, he'd say. Go wash your face and get dressed, son. It's pretty near afternoon. And I went to wash up and I could smell coffee perking on the gas stove all hot and brown-smelling and the blue eggs cracked and the yolks so yellow all stirred up and scrambled and the floor of the bathroom icy beneath my bare feet, the smell of Janet burning toast,

Dad stirring the eggs. I wet my hair and parted it down the middle, but I couldn't get the one cowlick flat and I put on my new jeans and old cowboy boots and my going-out shirt and tried to wet down my hair again but no, it just wouldn't stick. Janet, in her blue housecoat with one pocket ripped off so there is a square patch of darker blue where it used to be and Dad still smelling hay sweet of cow shit and and the sound of cream separating from milk downstairs. I ate two pieces of toast and eggs with ketchup and a cup of coffee because Dad was never one for making a fuss about age and what I could and couldn't do so as long as it was legal. Are you excited about your first day of school, son? he asked. Janet looked up from her toast dipped in sweet coffee, Sure glad it's you and not me. I only had to go 'til grade six in my time. Who knows, though. You might like it. Her hair was still mussy but a pretty brown colour with red shining. I dunno, I said, I guess so. But I must have been something because I had another cup of coffee. The bus came while it was still dark outside and I was the only one in it because we lived farthest out from anyone else who was going to school and we had to drive, me and the bus driver, for half an hour before anyone else got on, the driver, Ed, yawning five times, I counted. Finally getting light outside and stopped at the Lazy S Ranch to pick up the Samson sisters, but they were older kids and didn't even look at me, sitting in the very front, just slouched past to sit in the back. And we stopped more often, other ranches and farm houses and all the kids sitting in the back half of the bus and I learned that no one sits in the front through choice and there are a couple kids I knew from the odd wedding and 4-H cattle sales, but we were shy and too nervous to talk on the bus, getting closer to school and what kind of teacher would I get? Getting more nervous, the coffee in my gut all squishy sloshy and making me burp and I'd never gone to kindergarten because we lived too far out for me to come in, especially driven, for half a day of crayon and counting, and wishing I was at home sleeping between Dad and Janet on their lumpy bed smelling like homemade butter and sweet cow shit. We got to school and I waited until everyone got off first, then I just sorta followed everyone inside, only everyone dispersed to different rooms and I didn't know where I was supposed to be but I didn't want to ask a grown-up. The bell rang and I knew that meant I was supposed to be somewhere, so I just sidled into this room and it was full of bigger kids, sitting in desks, and a teacher with yellow hair and blue eyes bent down so his face was right above mine and smiled with yellow teeth. A few kids snickered and I heard someone said, I bet you he pees his pants. My face felt all hot and fat and my new jeans tight on my coffee tummy. The yellow man asked me in a too loud voice, What grade are you in? What's your name? I gulped, and said, Grade one. My name is Sun. The whole class room burst out laughing, and I heard one of the Samson sisters. That's funny, the yellow hair teacher said, that sounds like a Chinese name, but you don't look Chinese. Are you sure that's your name? Yes, I said firmly. Dad always calls me Sun. I see, said the teacher. And what's your father's name? Dad! of course, I said. Everyone was shrieking with laughter and my eyes felt all melty and my throat felt all hot and throbby. Even the teacher was laughing. Finally, he said, Son is not your name. It means a boy child. Your dad calls you son because he is your father. Dad means the same thing as father. Do you understand? And everything swung around and words and names all swirling and bang, they smacked into place so that something I had known and trusted was really a solid wall that I could run into and I puked my two cups of coffee and breakfast all over the teacher's shoes and Janet came to pick me up in the crew cab and I lay on the seat with my head in her lap and she patted my back."

He snubbed out his third cigarette and looked over at her. She was lying on her back, palms of her hands facing upward, her fingers slightly curled and relaxed. He thought she was asleep.

"So you don't have a name," she said, without opening her eyes.

"Something like that. I'm not even sure."

"You must be lonely."

"Only when I'm with other people."

"Are you lonely now?" she sat up and leaned against the headboard. Reached up for the cigarette tucked above her ear. He struck a match for her and shook it out instead of blowing.

"Not so bad with you. Your stories, they're something more than hollow shape and I can almost catch that feeling I had before my first day at school."

"You told a good story now," she thoughtfully tapped the ashes.

He smiled slowly.

"You keep changing, you know," she said. "Or how I translate you. I don't know who you are from one moment to the next. Are you still the same person who can *sukōshi* speak Japanese or was that something I made up on my own?"

He looked at her in amazement, his eyebrows raised, and eyes wide open.

"What do you mean? *Eigo hitotsu mo hanashitenal to omou kedo.* Haven't we been talking Japanese all along?"

Oh.

• • •

Murasaki

People always want to hear a happy story. Something with a warm-hearted ending with maybe a touch of a lesson that makes you think, yes, that was meaningful but very positive. Let's be more careful. People say this and that. Why can't you tell a story with a happy ending? Why do you have to be so sarcastic and depressing? It just depends on how you hear it. This is a happy story. Can't you tell? I've been smiling all along.

I went to Nanton by myself, and the first thing Mom asked me was if we had fought.

"No, Mom, we didn't fight. I wanted to come alone." I was sitting at the kitchen table, watching her bustle. "Mom, can you clean my ears?"

"Go get the *mimikaki* from your Obāchan's room," she said, setting the timer on the oven. Chicken cordon bleu, the freezer kind. I padded upstairs to Obāchan's room, still the same as the day she left. Kept clean by Mom for who knows why.

When I came down, Mom was already in the living room, sitting on the sunny side of the couch. She patted the cushion beside her and smiled with her eyes. When I came to stand beside her, she tugged my hand until I sat and gently pushed my shoulder until my head was snuggled in her warm soft lap. The scent of her clothes. The sun all roasty toasty on my face, my curled body.

"Mom?" I whispered.

"Yes, don't move."

"I'm going away soon," I said softly, so she might hear things unsaid.

"Yes, dear."

"Is that all you're going to say?"

"I've known it all along."

"Oh," I was slightly disappointed. Wanted a tearful mother, begging me to stay.

"You won't find her, you know. I couldn't even find her when we were in the same room," Mom said sensibly.

"I'm not looking. I'm just going, you know?"

"Not really, but I'll worry," Mom said. Softly, carefully, scratching the inside of my ear.

"I'll write," I said reassuringly.

"Is he going with you? I would feel better if he was," Mom sighed, knowing my answer before I even stated it.

"No. He just got here, but he has to arrive. You can't move on until you've arrived. I've finally arrived and now I can go."

"I really don't know what you're talking about. I arrived over thirty years ago."

"No, Mom. You're arriving still."

"According to you," she said sharply. "Using your own measure of standards."

"Yeah, you have a point."

"Stop nodding. I don't want to poke you."

"Sorry."

"Your father will miss you very much."

"He won't even notice I'm gone!"

"No. You just never noticed him noticing you. That's something of a flaw in your character, you know."

"Not like some people with no flaws at all," I muttered.

"And that's another," she added.

"What?"

"Your sarcasm. You'll never see anything if you're always busy being sarcastic."

"Words of wisdom from enlightened mother to impetuous young daughter."

"Not so young, either."

"Ouch!" I faked. Not my ear, but at Mom's words.

"Never mind. You go. Your father and I will stay here. Who knows, Obāchan might decide to drop by some time and I want to be here for that day. One postcard! All those words she had to say for so many years and she can only write one postcard! Well, those MasterCard receipts keep coming in, I suppose she must be well.

"You know, we could have traced her. All those receipts, we could have tracked her down. Why don't you?" I had my own reasons, but I didn't know what my Mom's were.

"Because her leaving meant she was strong enough to be happy. Strong enough to choose a direction. Because if she wanted to come back, she could. And I was happy for her. At least she's eating well. *Mattaku!* But I still hope you can do better than one postcard!"

"What did you say?"

"I said I hoped you'd be better about writing us."

"No, before that. Didn't you say '*Mattaku!*'?"

"I did no such thing!"

"Oh." Hmmmmm.

Two women take up two different roads, two different journeys at different times. They are not travelling with a specific destination in mind but the women are walking toward the same place. Whether they meet or not is not relevant.

This is not a mathematical equation.

I suppose there was a time when a body could travel with only a light backpack and a sturdy pair of shoes. Trade a bowl of soup and a slice of bread for a tale or two. If anybody could live that way, it would be Obāchan. Who knows, she may be doing exactly that and, even now, be putting words inside my mouth. Maybe it's time to start that practice again. I always have a pair of strong shoulders to work for my meals. But there must be a lot of people out there just starving for a filling story. Something that would leave a rich flavour on their tongue, on their lips. Lick, then suck their fingertips. Let me feed you.

There are people who say that eating is only a superficial means of understanding a different culture. That eating at exotic restaurants and oohing and aahing over the food is not even worth the bill paid. You haven't learned anything at all. I say that's a lie. What can be more basic than food itself? Food to begin to grow. Without it, you'd starve to death, even academics. But don't stop there, my friend, don't stop there, because food is the point of departure. A place where growth begins. You eat, you drink and you laugh out loud. You wipe the sweat off your forehead and take a sip of water. You tell a story, maybe two, with words of pain and desire. Your companion listens and listens, then offers a different telling. The waiter comes back with the main course and stays to tell his version. Your companion offers three more stories and the people seated at the next table lean over to listen. You push all the tables together and the room resounds with voices. You get dizzy and the ceiling tips, the chair melts beneath your body. You lie back on the ground and the world tilts, the words heaving in the air above you. You are drunk and it is oh so pleasurable.

"You can drop me off at Banff, if you would. Such a place, I've heard, I might as well see it."

"Let's make a date of it!" My cowboy friend grins at me with his sun-crinkled eyes, from beneath the brim of his creased hat.

"No," I say gently, "my journey is not yours and yours is not mine."

"But I thought. After last night and all. We might be spending some more time together, you know?"

"No. Last night was special. And something I was needing for a long time. But that doesn't mean I can stay, and you have your own journey to tend to."

"How will I see you again? At least a name or a phone number—"

"You will see me on every street, on every corner, in the semitrailer that passes your truck. I'll be that woman who picks up the dirty trays in the food fair at the zoo. I'll be the systems analyst in the office building you will some day go to work in. I'll be the teacher in the community centre when you go to learn the art of flower arrangement. You will pass me in Mac's and see me in Woolco and step on my foot at the race tracks. I will hover on the wind and in the leaves and dwell inside the soil beneath your feet. You will even hold me inside your body every time you breathe the air."

Ahh, the air is sweet with pine and sap. But cold! my nostril hairs are frozen brittle. He looked so sad, when he dropped me off, men with their affinity for unhappy endings! No need to make a tragedy out of every encounter. That doesn't mean I don't like to listen to Prokofiev's *Romeo and Juliet.* That I can't have a good cry after reading *Where the Red*

Fern Grows. But I'd rather hear a *mukashi-banashi* every time. Nothing like a good folk legend to warm up one's belly and fill the emptiness inside you. Why a good folk tale can keep you going for at least a month, none of this manna talk and birds falling out of the sky.

But what a strange place Banff is, surrounded by jagged peaks of rock and ice, filled with the clamour of Japanese voices. Why, in the stores and restaurants, the signs are written in *katakana.* Who would have thought, this centre of snow and wind, and not a single cicada pupa sleeping beneath the soil, I'm certain. Funny how tourists flock from Japan in organized groups only to another translation of their home. With false fronts from Germany and Switzerland. It's a funny thing and you can never be sure if you're here or there. I carry my home in the cup of my palms, in the small hollows of my mouth. This is no place for a woman like me to stay. Let me travel from story to story.

"Mom," I asked.

"Yes?"

"Could you tell me about our last name?"

"What do you want to know? You should ask your Dad, he would know more about it after all. You still have talk to him, don't you?"

"Yeah, I suppose." There could always be a first. "Where is he?"

"Where else? In his office at the farm."

The grasshoppers whirred away from my feet and the sun-dry heat scorched the top of my head. I always wondered if the sun was hot enough, if my black hair would hold enough heat for me to fry an egg. I suppose not, if I were still alive. But, the thought interested me for a time in my childhood.

I crunched the gravel drive, and when I walked past the compost barn the pigeons roared away in a sudden flurry, their wings heavy with compost moisture. They nested in the ceiling of the barn, and every year the shit got deeper and heavier. Sometimes, when I was younger, I'd go out and blast them with a shot gun on my days off. But my urge to kill things started ebbing away, the older I grew. Watching gophers explode didn't seem much fun after a few summers. Dad never killed anything. Even when there was the danger of twenty years of pigeon shit caving in the ceiling. And no one was signing up to clean it out either. Dad just reinforced the walls and put up a couple steel pillars in the middle of the barn. Not that there was ever enough money to fix it. There was only money enough to keep the farm going and pay everyone's wages. And pay for Obāchan's credit card bills.

Can was outside getting a tank of propane for the forklift. Looked up at the roaring pigeons.

"Hi, girl. What are you doing?"

"I'm just coming around to say goodbye. I'm going away."

"Where are you going to?"

"I don't know for sure. I'll know when I get there."

"You're a funny girl. When you were little, you hated me, huh?"

"Yeah, I guess I did. I'm sorry about things."

"Ohhh, you hate me, you like me, it doesn't make a difference. It's difficult to talk of things when you're young. We can talk now, huh?"

"Yeah, thank you. Yeah, I would really like that."

"You going back to Calgary tonight?"

"No, I'm sleeping over, then going in the morning."

"Then come over tonight. We should drink together before you go. So nothing makes you look back and feel bitterness."

"Thanks, Can. I would really like that a lot. Do you think you could tell me some stories?"

"Sure. Sure. See you tonight, then, Murasaki. Your dad, he's in his office."

Bemused. I was bemused. I slipped sideways through the little door in the wall, the bottom of the door frame a good two feet off the ground. Even I had to duck my head to get inside the door. Why was this door so small? Why didn't I ever ask? The Green Machine was clean and had been sprayed with formaldehyde to kill any diseases, molds, or mites. I covered my nose and mouth with my forearm and squinted my eyes into slits. Tears made it impossible to see, I hadn't been there for quite a while and I wasn't acclimatized. I bumped into someone, "Sorry."

"Muriel."

"Huh, Dad?" I said, peering above my arm.

"Nice to see you."

"Thanks."

"Come into my office. It's not so bad in there."

I followed Dad into his room. For the first time in my life. Funny, I wondered, why hadn't I ever seen it before? It was surprisingly neat and the plywood floor was raised so that water on the main concrete wouldn't seep inside the office. There was a high power fm/am radio playing classical music. I never knew. And the walls of the room, they were covered with shelves, filled with books and books.

Hundreds and thousands and quadruple that, they towered all around making me dizzy. There was even a step ladder in the corner to reach the ones on top. I sank back into a chair. Dad looked sheepish, and I felt red crawl up my neck. The books were all in Japanese.

"Why—you knew all along! How could you?! When you knew that I wanted to learn. All along, you knew, and you didn't say a word." Without knowing it, I was standing up, my hands clenched into fists. Dad looked sternly at my hands, and I noticed my own violence. I unclenched my fists and sank back into the chair.

"All along, all along. God, you must really hate me."

"That's always been your worst fault, you know. Thinking the worst of people who love you. Without asking why. My teaching you nothing Japanese had nothing to do with you. And I was very proud of you when you decided to learn it yourself. No, the problem was all mine."

"Why, then?" I felt like crying and felt stupid for feeling like crying. "Finally, why didn't you teach me to speak Japanese?"

"Because I couldn't."

"Because of Mom? She forbade you to do it?" I demanded.

"See, there you go again! I don't know how you came to be so distrustful. Well, I guess we're not innocent either—"

"Tell me!"

"It's because I cannot speak it, Muriel. I cannot speak it at all. I can only read it to understand."

"Really?" I said doubtfully. "Is that really possible?"

"I don't know if it's a medical condition. But it's my reality. When we moved to Canada, your Mom and I, we decided it would be best for our children if we let them slip in with everybody èlse. Sure, we couldn't change the colour of their hair, or the shape of their face, but we could make sure they didn't stand out. That they could be as Canadian as everyone around them. As it turned out, you were the only child we had, and that made us even more careful. We wanted only your happiness. We decided, your Mom and I, that we would put Japan behind us and fit more smoothly with the crowd. And from that day, when we decided, neither of us could speak a word in Japanese. Not a word would pass our lips. We couldn't even think it. And I was ashamed. I felt a loss so fine it pierced my heart. Made it ache. So I stopped talking. I used to talk a lot in my youth, that's what won your Mom to me. She was taken with my chatter and my jokes. But after the day I lost my words, my home words, I didn't have the heart to talk so much. I just put my energies into the farm, grew mushrooms in the quiet of the dark. Kay put it all behind her. She has a strong will, your Mom, so she just said, that's fine. That's life then. And carried on like nothing happened. We don't talk about it. Some things, you don't talk about. And I was feeling like I was half missing for a good ten years, never mixing with other Japanese folk, the communities in Calgary and Lethbridge, because it made the ache unbearable. Even if the third or fourth generation Japanese-Canadians could speak only English, like me, it wasn't the same. They weren't half a person like I was. Then this Japanese-Canadian minister from Lethbridge, I hardly met him once, he sent me a copy of *The New Canadian.* It's a newspaper out of Vancouver, I think. Or maybe Toronto. Half is in English and the other half in Japanese. I picked it up and couldn't help myself, I glanced at the characters written there. And I could read it! I could read it and understand!

But when I tried to say it out loud, there was nothing. Still, I was so happy. So happy. I called your Mom to tell her the news, but she said it was too late for her. And it was too late for you. That she didn't want to stir things up when it was all settled. So I didn't push it. And I wouldn't have been able to teach you even if your Mom had allowed it. The words were only inside my head to read, not something I could speak. I'm sorry Muriel, that's why I can't call you by the name your grandmother gave you, why I taught you nothing. I guess I'm not innocent after all. I guess I could have sent you to Calgary for special lessons. Your Mom is strong-willed, Muriel, and I went along with her decision. And I love her still. I hope you can forgive me."

Dad sank into a chair, his face so pale. I had never heard so many words come out of my his mouth at one time. I poured him a cup of muddy water that was sitting in the coffee maker. He gulped it back and wiped his mouth and forehead with a piece of toilet paper. I sighed.

"I'm sorry too. Sorry too."

We sat in the blue hum of fluorescent lights.

"What about our name? Isn't our name Japanese?"

Dad actually laughed, and it was a dirt brown sound.

"It's funny, really. That word. It was the only word I could utter when the change took place. Your Mom suggested we take a Canadian name, if we couldn't remember our real one. But I was firm about that. I said if we couldn't remember our own name, the least we could do was keep the one word I could remember. Tonkatsu! Of all things!" Dad started laughing so hard that tears were rolling down his cheeks.

"Does our name really mean 'breaded deep fried pork cutlets'?"

"The translation isn't literal as that, but that's what it signifies. The thing is, *tonkatsu* isn't really a purely Japanese word. *Ton,* meaning pork, is Japanese, but *katsu* is adopted from 'cutlet', and I don't know the origins of that word."

"That's really weird, Dad."

"So the joke is on us, really. I don't know why I only remembered *tonkatsu,* but that's what our name became. You can always change yours, if you like. It's not a binding thing for you."

"I don't know, I might keep it. Keep me from forgetting my humble past and all that."

"Well, you do what you like. I guess you always have," he said, and tugged the end of my nose. I laughed.

"Actually, that's why I came to see you. I'm going away. And I wanted to let you know."

"Glad to hear it!" Dad winked.

"Really?"

"Of course. Plenty out there. Plenty more than just living in Calgary for the rest of your life. Or Nanton for that matter. Your mother and I, we left Japan and came to be in Nanton. I suppose it's reasonable that you need to find elsewhere. Whatever or wherever it happens to be. Are you going overseas?"

"No, I don't want to be a tourist. And nothing so biblical as a mission. There is a sound I can almost hear, just slightly outside my hearing range. And I want to know what that sound is. What I'm missing. That's about as close as I can get."

"Are you going to Japan?"

"No, no. That's too literal a translation, I think."

"Well, wherever you go, you write your Mom and me

so we don't have to worry."

"Sure, Dad. I can do that. I'll be writing all the time."

"Did I hear Joe inviting you over for a drink?"

"Yeah."

"Do you think I could join you if Joe doesn't mind."

"Dad, I'd really like that."

Dad swung his office door wide, and we stepped out. The formaldehyde had lifted or evaporated, or whatever it does, and my eyes didn't water any longer.

An Immigrant Story With a Happy Ending

Mukāshi, mukāshi, ōmukashi . . .

Why do you leave a homeland in the first place? If there isn't any turmoil and plenty of food and political freedom to top it off, why would anyone ever leave? And if you don't like the way the new country treats you, why would you bother to stay?

"I *deserve* to be here. I *earned* the right to live here. Those other people, who knows where they came from? That's why there is a gang problem. They didn't come through the right channels. When I came here, I was questioned and interviewed and they made sure of my intent. I provided new jobs for the people here and I've never ever been on welfare. Not like some others. We carry their load on our backs. I say we should never let them in."

"You can never trust those people, you know. Heavens, I've tried, but you can never tell what they're thinking. And they always stick to their own kind, never mixing with other people. Always talking in a foreign language. And even when they do bother talking in English, why their accent is so thick, I can't make out a single word. If those people want to live in Canada, they've got to try a little harder. That's not too much to ask, is it?"

"Have you seen *Mr Baseball?* It's about this American baseball player who goes to Japan to play because he isn't good enough to play in the States and he doesn't understand the culture at all and he causes a lot of trouble on the team until he finally learns to live with the culture rather than against it? It was really funny. You ought to go see it."

"Chinese, Japanese, dirty knees, look at these!"
(Pinch a bit of material from your shirt about breast level with both hands and pull outward so that you make two cloth pyramids haha.)

When does it end?When does itend?When doesitend?When doesitendWhendoesitendwhendoesitendwhendoesitendwhendoesitendwhendoesitendwhendoesitendwhen

You tell me.

An immigrant story with a happy ending. Nothing is impossible. Within reason, of course.

When does one thing end and another begin?

Can you separate the two?

PART FIVE

"Laaaaadies and gentlemen, the event you've all been waitin' for! It's time for the meanest, toughest cowboys on two thousand pounds of lean muscle and grit. Let's give a rowdy Calgary Stampede yaaahoooo to the best bullriders in the whole, wide world!"

"Yaaaaaaaaahooooooooooooo!"

Easy enough for a woman to slip by security. If you're quietly Oriental and carrying a *furoshiki* packed with cowboy equipment and starkers as the day you were born, people are glad not to notice you. Like telling people you were picked up by alien life forms and impregnated on a distant planet. If you mentioned what you saw, you'd be the one bundled away. In a soft-cushioned van with wire mesh over the windows.

A winter away from Alberta is pure pleasure, but funny how a glancing memory of an unappetizing corndog is enough to tug you back to Calgary in time for the Stampede. I don't know why, when there is a International Jazz Festival in Montreal and unmanned light shows surpassing imagination in the Arctic. So why do I swing by, this annual migration, to catch a rodeo? Spin on the Zipper and watch

Elvis impersonations? *Mattaku!* There's not an answer for everything, that's certain. No harm in a body going to see a rodeo once a year, I say. No harm in participating. Why, the best place to be is behind the chutes, where you can smell the adrenalin sweat of young and old cowboys alike. The sweet smell of horsehide and green grass sweat. Sour mash shit and hot dogs and coffee.

I hunker down between a couple of horse trailers and get my equipment out of my *furoshiki.* My calfskin boots, my bat wing chaps, my bull rope with two cow bells. Work glycerine and rosin, with my thumb, into the braid of the rope where I will grip. The rosin smells pine sharp and strong as trees. I pull on my jeans and tuck in my shirt. Tie my soft boots on snug so they won't fly off when I spur. Get out my purple mask from the pocket of my jeans and cover my eyes. Like that other masked wonder, who rode that Hi Ho Silver horse, I can't remember his name. Buckle up chaps, top myself off with a well-worn Stetson and finally, tug my riding glove on my left hand. Shoulder my bull rope, all coiled up and walk back to the chutes. Cowboys, cowgirls, they leave me room, and I can hear them murmur.

"The Purple Mask! The Purple Mask! The Purple Mask is here!"

Some nod their heads, some tip their hats, and others scowl and spit. When you do something different, not everyone will like you, I've noticed. Ahhh, I say, nothing an old woman can't manage.

"Ladies and gentlemen! I've just received a special bulletin. There's word that The Purple Mask has been seen near the chutes! Now for those of you who've never heard of The Purple Mask, you folks from out of town, The Purple Mask is a mysteeeerious bullrider who shows up at the Calgary Stampede and gives bullriding a whole new meaning. No one knows who he is, where he comes from. He doesn't even have a pro card. But lordy, can he ride! He just showed up one year and he's been coming around ever since. Only takes one ride. Never had a wreck. Plumb mysterious. The Purple Mask is a legend in these parts come Stampede time, and you're going to get your money's worth when you see this cowboy ride!"

"Who did I draw?" I ask, before I slip my mouth guard in.

"You drew Revelation," a cowboy nods. "He's a bit rank today."

I tug the brim of my hat, walk up to my bull. Revelation! *Mattaku!* Such a name for a bull! Why he is brindled, all tiger-striped. Such nasty eyes on his lamb-white face. He snaps his back hoof at my foot when I climb up the side of the chute, and I pull it back so quick he clangs only metal. I dangle my rope down the inside, beside the bull, and the man opposite, he hooks it under and pulls it up over the back. I straddle the bull's body, my feet still standing on the chute and slip the tail of the rope through the loop and pull it tight. The cowboy who caught up the rope, he leans down to yank up any slack and I pull it tight again. I gingerly lower my body onto the bull. Settle my riding hand, holding the rope with my palm facing upward, and wrap the rope up and around the back of my hand and the tail back into my palm. Fling the trailing end of it toward the front so that a bullfighter can pull it loose if I'm thrown off, away from my hand, and get hung up on the beast. Pound my clenched fist with my free hand, *ichi, ni,* making sure it's secure. Settle my weight above my hand, so that my butt isn't touching. I'm holding my body up with the inside of my thighs. The nervous heat of the bull seeping through the straps on my chaps, the rough cotton of my jeans. My shoulders just over the centre of my clenched riding fist. Stretch out my strong arm, shoulder level, and reach for balance. I nod my head.

The gate is pulled open from the outside, but the bull crashes it to get out faster. Clang of horns on metal. The first lurch is shocking, like always, and I push against the rope so I won't fly over the bull's head, his curving horns. He lurches upward and twists into a belly roll and I pull back to keep my position. The clang clang of cowbells only a dim sound in the pounding of heart and heaving pant of animal breath. The brine of his sweat, the lean muscles of his back. He lunges on and dives into a sunfish. I push and pull, my strong arm reaching for that place of balance.

"Woweee! Lookit that cowboy ride! This is where the world meets the West! This is what the Greatest Show on Earth is all about! Hang in there, partner, hang in there, cowboy! This is the ride of your life! Eeeeeeeehaaa!"

Can't hear the crowds or the rodeo announcer. The sound all muffled into background. Only the bull and me, never partners, but never really enemies. My head tucked low and my strong hand reaching. Just reaching for that place. That place of comfort, of safety, where I can float like a ballerina, like a Minoan gymnast. For that place where the bull and I can move as one. The jolt and lurch in my arm and spine, ahhh, this old woman can hold on still. Revelation twists into a lurching spin, and I ride into a storm. A funnel forms from where we spin and spreads outward with dust and howling. Blowing blowing spinning round and cowboy hats swirl in dizzy circles. Cotton candy fills the air, and people duck flying corn on the cob or are splattered with wet smacks of grease and salt. We spin tighter, tighter, an infinite source of wind and dust. The roaring howl of dust devil turned tornado. The wind we churn flings cowboy hats to Winnipeg, Victoria, Montreal, as far as Charlottetown. Weather patterns will be affected for the next five years and no one will know the reason. It makes me laugh and I'm still riding, the bull is still beneath me.

And I find it. I find it. That smooth clear space where the animal and I are pure as light as sound. Where stars turn liquid and you can taste sweet nectar in your mouth. The glide of the animal in your heart and in your lungs and the very blood of your body. Heat of the bull between your legs, riding on a crest of power. Tension and pleasure as fine as a silken thread. The moment of such sweet purity, it brings tears to your throat, your eyes. Makes your lips tremble.

"Thank you," I say. Because it is a difficult thing to hear. And harder still, to listen. You shake your head and smile. Touch my hair, my face, just so.

I rise from our great purple futon like someone who has been sleeping for decades. Step through the open door. Away from a room filled with the lingering echoes of spoken and unspoken tales.

You know you can change the story.

Texts that influenced the writing of this novel:

Dorson, Richard M. *Folk Legends of Japan.* Japan: Charles E. Tuttle Co. Inc., 1981.

Piggott, Julie. *Japanese Mythology.* New York, NY: Peter Bedrick Books, 1991.

Shikibu, Muraskai. *The Tale of Genji.* 2 vols. Translated with an Introduction by Edward G. Seidensticker. Japan: Charles E. Tuttle Co. Inc., 1991.

Hiromi Goto

Hiromo Goto was born in 1966 in Chiba-ken, Japan, and immigrated to Canada at the age of three with her family. After a short time on the West Coast, they moved to southern Alberta. Hiromi graduated with a BA degree in English from the University of Calgary in 1989. She lives in Calgary.